W9-BZT-249

# THE BOY WHO LOVED
# ALLIGATORS

# THE BOY WHO LOVED ALLIGATORS

## BARBARA KENNEDY

**A JEAN KARL BOOK**

ATHENEUM 1994 NEW YORK

*Maxwell Macmillan Canada*
TORONTO
*Maxwell Macmillan International*
NEW YORK • OXFORD • SINGAPORE • SYDNEY

Copyright © 1994 by Barbara Kennedy

All rights reserved. No part of this book may be reproduced or transmitted in any form or by any means, electronic or mechanical, including photocopying, recording, or by any information storage and retrieval system, without permission in writing from the Publisher.

Atheneum
Macmillan Publishing Company
866 Third Avenue
New York, NY 10022

Maxwell Macmillan Canada, Inc.
1200 Eglinton Avenue East
Suite 200
Don Mills, Ontario M3C 3N1

Macmillan Publishing Company is part of
the Maxwell Communication Group of Companies.

First edition

Printed in the United States of America

The text of this book is set in Caslon 224.

10 9 8 7 6 5 4 3 2 1

Library of Congress Cataloging-in-Publication Data
Kennedy, Barbara, 1925–
    The boy who loved alligators / Barbara Kennedy. —1st ed.
        p.    m.
    "A Jean Karl book."
    Summary: After moving to Orlando, Florida, and befriending an alligator because he considers it to be as ugly and unwanted as he is, Jim starts to feel different about his life.
    ISBN 0-689-31876-6
    [1. Alligators—Fiction. 2. Self-esteem—Fiction. 3. Florida—Fiction.]
I. Title.
PZ7.K377Bo    1994
[Fic]—dc20                                              93-15982

# CHAPTER 1

**W**ho's going to take the kid?" Aunt Bessie Klinger asked. She was old and ugly, with a deep harsh voice, and not his aunt. Jim Allengood liked her.

There was silence from the six other people gathered in Aunt Bessie's living room, eating from paper plates balanced on their knees. Occasionally they got up to refill their plates from the food on the kitchen table. Neighbors had brought in potato salad, rice with sausage, two cakes, and a bowl of fruit and Jell-O.

Jim didn't include himself when he counted the six people. People were adults. He was a kid of thirteen, Martha Schott's grandson who had just been to her funeral in his Sunday jeans and a clean T-shirt and his only shoes, a pair of black high-tops.

"Go get yourself some cake, kid," Aunt Bessie said. She always called him kid.

Obediently Jim took his paper plate into the kitchen, knowing that he was being sent away so that they could talk about him. He stood at the kitchen table, pretending to study the food, straining to hear what they were saying. They kept their voices down, but there was no door between the kitchen and the living room, only an archway painted yellow like the walls. Aunt Bessie liked bright colors.

He heard her say, "I'm too old, I'm going to die soon." Jim didn't think she was too old. Anybody who could keep him in this little frame house, on this narrow street, in this old neighborhood, here in Tampa, in Florida, wasn't too old. If Aunt Bessie could hang in for three more years, until he was sixteen, then he could make it on his own.

Madeline, the heavyset woman with red hair, said in her squeaky voice that she had too many kids of her own.

Then Fred said, "I might take him back, only he better straighten out this time."

Jim heard his heart beating inside his chest. He could still feel the lash of Fred's belt from the time he'd lived with him. He was only five then. Grandma took him to live with her in Aunt Bessie's house because she couldn't stand the way Fred treated him.

"I wouldn't send a dog to live with you, Fred," Aunt Bessie said. "What about you, Billie? You have a house, don't you?"

Billie lived in Orlando. Jim tensed as he waited for her to answer.

"A house and two mortgages and no man," she

said. Her voice was short and sharp. "A boy that age needs a man."

"I said I'd take him," Fred muttered.

"He's a good kid, Billie," Aunt Bessie said. "He never gave Martha no back talk, me neither. She was all crippled up with arthritis, used to say he was her legs. He did the running for both of us."

"I can't take him," Billie said. "I'm working two jobs just to pay my bills."

"He does real well in school," Aunt Bessie coaxed. "I'd let him stay here, but I can't keep up with this house anymore. I'd have sold it and gone to a home a long time ago, only if I did where would Martha go? She didn't have anybody but me."

"I have two kids of my own," Billie said. "I can't take on any more."

"Clara?"

"Honey, if I go back to Alabama with another kid, my husband's going to lock the door on me!"

"Annabelle?"

"Uh-uh." The negative sound came from Randall, Annabelle's husband. "I'm fixin' to retire in three years. I'm not about to start raisin' kids again."

"I know he's homely," Aunt Bessie said, "but he's a real good kid. He won't give you a bit of trouble."

There it was, the real reason nobody wanted him. Aunt Bessie had said homely, but Jim knew that he was ugly. He was too thin, his ears stuck out, and his hair, a crew cut grown out into a shag, was a horrible bright ginger color. His eyelashes were so pale you could hardly see them, and he wore glasses. This year he grew so tall that he was in size sixteens, which were two sizes too wide. He kept his head down and avoided mirrors. Nobody liked an ugly kid.

Fred came out to the kitchen to refill his plate. He was a harmless-looking man, going bald, with mild blue eyes and skin the color of dirty sand. Today he was wearing a navy blue suit. As he looked at Jim his mouth spread in a smile that said, Oh boy, just wait till I get you back.

Jim felt his whole body stiffen. If Fred got him, he'd run away the first night and live on the streets. While they were staring at each other, Billie came into the kitchen. She was fairly old, Jim guessed, around thirty, with dark hair to her shoulders.

He knew from the look on her face that she'd seen Fred's ugly smile, although the moment she appeared Fred changed his expression. Billie glared at him. He flushed and went back into the living room.

Behind his glasses Jim squinted his eyes, then averted them as Billie looked at him. She poured a cup of coffee and rejoined the adults. Jim heard her say, "What happens if nobody takes him?"

"I guess I'll have to call the HRS, let them find him a foster home," Aunt Bessie said. "Martha didn't let them know she had him. She was afraid they'd say she was too old and take him away."

Jim knew all about the HRS—the Department of

Health and Rehabilitative Services. They took kids like him, who had no parents, or bad parents, and put them in foster homes.

"They wouldn't let Fred have him, would they?" Billie asked.

"You never know what they'll do," Aunt Bessie said.

"If it looked like he was going to get him," Billie said, "I'd come down here and tell them what happened when he had him before."

"If you could just take him for the summer, I could make sure he goes to his daddy's folks," Aunt Bessie coaxed.

"He needs a family," Billie said.

"I could find him one," Aunt Bessie said eagerly. "I'll write his daddy's cousins in Georgia; they'll just love to have that boy! But I'm putting my house up for sale, I need to find a place for him right now." There was a short silence. "He's a good kid," Aunt Bessie said.

"What if I'm ready to bring him back and you've sold your house?"

"Honey, by then I'll have him all lined up to go to Georgia! You taking him will give me time to do that!"

"I can't keep him longer than the summer," Billie warned. "My girls are with their father, but they'll be back when school starts."

"That will be just fine," Aunt Bessie cried. "I'll start tonight finding out his daddy's folks' address."

Jim knew how her mind worked. She thought that by the end of the summer he'd have made himself so useful that Billie wouldn't want to part with him. Optimism came naturally to her and Grandma. It didn't seem to matter that they didn't get what they wanted very often. By the time one expectation fizzled out, they'd moved on to others.

It was contagious. He felt his own hope stirring, that he'd get along with Billie and she'd want to keep him. Anything was better than living with Fred.

# CHAPTER 2

**H**e'd never been on a superhighway. Grandma and Aunt Bessie had no car. Sometimes Rick Green's father took Rick and Jim in his truck, but only to the movies or the neighborhood shopping center. The wide lanes arching over the city dazzled him. He sucked in his breath and fantasized that he was Superman.

Billie drove her old gray Dodge Dart fast, and changed lanes often. The city buildings fell behind them. Cement gave way to grass. She drove without speaking, heading north, in the fast lane. Flat land stretched away on either side, dotted with scrawny pine trees and palmettos. Jim read the green-and-white road signs. Lakeland 10, Orlando 62. The excitement of the journey made him want to talk.

"Miss Billie?"

"Mmm?"

"I'm sure glad you're letting me live with you."

"I wasn't about to let that creep Fred have you," Billie said grimly. "Your grandma told me how he treated you when you lived with him before. And don't you worry you might end up with him when you go back, because I won't let it happen, hear?"

"Yes ma'am."

"It's not him that's related to you anyway, it was his wife, and she got a divorce and moved away."

She fell silent again. Grandma and Aunt Bessie had talked all the time, in a series of questions, so that he was saying "Yes ma'am" and "No ma'am" all day.

He screwed up his courage to speak again. "Miss Billie?"

"Mmm?"

"How'd you know my grandma?"

"I grew up in Tampa, she was my grandmother's cousin, they were good friends. Aunt Bessie called me, told me she had a heart attack, died."

Aunt Bessie had taken his grandma's book, where she kept important information, including his birth certificate in an envelope just inside the cover. She sat beside the telephone with the book in her lap, after the ambulance came for his grandma, and called the relatives.

"I went out of respect," Billie said. "We didn't see each other for years, but we kept in touch. She wrote me every Christmas, and I called her once in a while."

"Fred said she wasn't really my grandma."

"She was in your mama's family. It don't matter what folks are, it's how they treat you."

"Did you know my mama?"

"A long time ago, when I was a kid, we had family reunions. I used to see her there."

"Grandma said she was real pretty."

"She was real sweet," Billie said. "That's better than pretty."

Jim hesitated, then said, "You're real pretty, Miss Billie."

"That and fifty cents'll get me a cup of coffee," Billie snapped.

There was another lengthy silence. They passed the entrance to Walt Disney World. Jim had never been there. The green road sign said Orlando 18. They were getting close to home. That was how he thought of it, this place he'd never seen. He had to believe that he was going from one home to another.

As if Billie could read his thoughts, she said, "I can only keep you for the summer. Then you'll have to go back. But I won't let Fred have you."

"Yes ma'am."

"You'll go back before then if you give me any trouble. I work two jobs, I'm gone a lot, you'll be on your own. You better behave yourself."

"Yes ma'am. Did you say you have two kids?"

"Two girls. They're with their father in Atlanta for the summer. I'm divorced."

"Yes ma'am."

She turned off the highway before they got into the city of Orlando, and drove along a two-lane country road. Apartments and houses appeared, interspersed with strips of shops, and then a housing area

9

identified by black letters on a white cement block wall as Hidden Grove. Billie turned into it on a street named Orange Blossom Lane. The houses were different colors, with short front lawns. Jim thought they were palatial.

She pulled into the drive of a house painted white with black trim. A lack of plants and flowers made it look barer than the others. Jim hardly noticed; it was much newer, and in a younger neighborhood, than Aunt Bessie's old frame house.

"This is a real nice house," he said.

"Too bad I'm about to lose it," Billie snapped.

He was afraid to ask why. Inside the house it was warm. Billie operated a switch on the wall. "I'll get us some air," she said.

He'd never lived in a house with central air-conditioning. The floor was carpeted in a deep rose color, and the furniture was covered in lighter shades that Grandma and Aunt Bessie would have said were hard to keep up. The TV set was in a separate room, where everything looked older. Billie led him down a hallway into a room with twin beds and a double dresser. There were pink roses on the bedspreads, and dolls and stuffed animals piled in the corners.

"I rent out the third bedroom," Billie said. "I have an ad in the paper now for a roomer. Last one I had drank, I had to get rid of her. This is my girls' room. They come home, you'll have to go back to Tampa."

"Yes ma'am." He knew that she kept mentioning it

so that he couldn't say, when she sent him back, that he didn't know about it.

She opened a drawer in the double dresser and put what was in there into another one. "You can put your stuff in here, and there's plenty of room in the closet. The girls took about everything they had with them." She opened the closet door; all he could see in there were a lot of empty hangers and a couple of hooded winter jackets.

"Yes ma'am."

"These are my kids." Billie pointed to two school photos in frames. "This is Lorraine, she's ten, and this is Jennifer, she just had her fourteenth birthday."

Lorraine was blond and chubby, with curly hair and a big smile. Jennifer was thinner, with long dark hair like Billie's.

"They're cute," Jim said. "Who are the other pictures?" There was one of a middle-aged man and woman, and another of a man with a mustache, a bit like Tom Selleck.

"That's my mother and dad, and the girls' father," Billie said. "My mom died when I was in my teens, then my daddy was killed in an automobile accident. I have a brother in Texas, but I don't get to see him much."

Jim nodded and surveyed his surroundings once more. "This is a real nice room," he said.

"I expect you to keep it picked up, hear? The

house too. I don't want to come home from work and find a big mess and the sink full of dirty dishes."

"No ma'am." He hesitated, then said, "I did all the housework for Grandma." Suddenly there were tears in his eyes. He turned away to hide them.

"You thought a lot of your grandma, didn't you?" Billie asked. He nodded, and felt his tears drop to the rug. "It's okay to cry," Billie said. "There's nothing wrong with crying for someone you loved. You have a picture of her, maybe of your mama and daddy, you want to put out?"

"No ma'am. I don't have any pictures."

She left him alone. He wiped his face on his T-shirt, and opened the old suitcase Aunt Bessie had given him. In the drawer Billie had emptied he made three piles of his four T-shirts, two pairs of jeans, two pairs of underwear, and three pairs of socks. He put his comic books on top of a bookcase filled with books and stuffed animals, and his empty suitcase under the bed. Then he changed from his good clothes into old jeans and an old T-shirt.

Through the wall came the sound of a shower and of drawers opening and closing. He sat on one of the beds and read his comic books until Billie came back, wearing a black skirt and white blouse.

"I hate to do this to you, but I have to go to work," she said. "I waitress nights at Carlo's Steakhouse. Come on and I'll write down the number, but you only call me in a real emergency, hear?"

Jim followed her through the house into a small

kitchen with pink striped wallpaper. While she wrote down the telephone number she gave him his instructions for the night. He could make himself a sandwich when he got hungry. He was to stay in the house and lock the door. He could watch television, but she wanted him in bed at ten o'clock. If anybody came to the door, he was to pretend there was nobody home.

"What if they hear the TV?" he asked.

"That's okay, just don't open the door. You get scared, you call this second number, that's the Toths next door. If the phone rings, don't say you're here by yourself. Say I'm busy and I'll call them back."

She showed him how to operate the television set. The house was very quiet after she left.

# CHAPTER 3

He watched the shows he'd always watched with Grandma and Aunt Bessie, and went to bed at ten o'clock. In the morning he woke up to bright sunshine through the flowered curtains. There was no sound behind the closed door of Billie's room. He set two places at the table in the dining area and reread all his comic books. Then he read a book from the bookcase in the girls' room. It was all about girls; he'd never read anything like it before.

It was close to noon when he heard sounds from Billie's room. While he was running water into a kettle at the sink, she came out in a terry-cloth robe, with fuzzy hair, and no makeup on her pale skin.

"I'm making you some coffee," Jim said. The jar of instant Maxwell House, which he'd found in a cupboard, stood on the counter.

Billie looked startled. "Thanks," she said; then, "It's quicker in the microwave." She showed him which buttons to punch on the microwave oven. "How'd you get along last night?" she asked.

14

"Okay. I watched TV, went to bed ten o'clock like you said." The microwave beeped. Jim removed the red mug covered with white polka dots and handed it to her.

"Thanks," Billie said. "I'll take it on back to my room, get dressed."

When she returned she was wearing white shorts and a yellow shirt, with her dark hair twisted on top of her head. She fried a can of corned beef hash and broke two eggs into it.

"This is the meal of the day," she warned. "We'll have a sandwich tonight before I go to work."

"You work Sundays?"

"I work every day since I had to put a new roof on the house last winter. That was over four thousand dollars. I'm still paying it off."

"Yes ma'am."

He helped her clean up after the meal. She had a dishwasher, but said that she never used it, to save on her electric bill. Then she offered to show him the neighborhood. They went outside into the hot June sun.

Billie walked in the opposite direction from the road they'd turned off yesterday. There was nobody out on Orange Blossom Lane. The air-conditioning motors hummed in the hot moist air. The short street dead-ended on a dirt road. On the far side there were tall trees and ragged bushes; directly opposite where they stood was a sandy driveway and a white frame house partly hidden by tall shrubs.

15

"This used to be out in the country when we bought here ten years ago," Billie said. She pointed down the dirt road. "They're building down there, and"—pointing in the other direction—"they just sold the orange grove down there. Pretty soon it'll be all houses, and they'll pave the street."

"Who lives over there?" Jim indicated the house across the street.

"That's old Mr. Morrison. Don't you go bothering him, hear?"

"No ma'am."

"Some of the kids around here think it's smart to play tricks on him. You leave him alone, stay on your own side of the street."

"Yes ma'am."

"There's a lake over there, nasty dirty place, all weeds, you stay out of it. You want to go swimming, I'll see can I get you a ride to the municipal pool with the other kids."

"I can't swim."

"Every kid in Florida should know how to swim."

They walked back to her house in the bright hot sunshine. Jim, who had lived in Florida since he was a baby, liked the feel of it on his arms. Even the sweat growing like moss on his body had a comfortable feeling, now that he knew he was going back into air-conditioning. As they walked up the drive Billie said, "I used to have an orange tree in my backyard. It died in the freeze two years ago, my shrubs and flowers too. I didn't replace them. I don't have the time or the money anymore."

Back in the house, she called her daughters in Atlanta. He heard her tell them that she had a relative staying with her, a thirteen-year-old boy from Tampa. "It's nice," she said. "I was real lonely without you two." There was a pause, then she said, "Just till August. I can't keep him after that." Jim went to his room; he didn't need to be reminded again that he wasn't going to stay here very long.

He read for the rest of the afternoon, until Billie called him to eat the lunch-meat sandwiches she'd made. She was in her work clothes. "Garbage pickup's tomorrow," she said. "I want you to put the can out on the curb before you go to bed. Don't forget."

"No ma'am."

She reminded him of all the rules she'd laid down the day before, then putt-putted away in her old car. That night he couldn't get to sleep, and heard her come in late. In the morning he woke to the distant sound of the shower. He got up and made a mug of coffee. There were sounds from the carpeted hallway of someone in a hurry, then Billie rushed out.

"I'm running late, I—oh." She looked startled as Jim held out the coffee. "Thanks," she said. "I'll take it with me." She had her car keys in her hand. "There's cereal in the cupboard. No kids in the house, and you don't go in anybody else's house unless the parents are there, hear? I'll see you tonight."

17

Jim followed her into the carport. "Where do you work?" he asked.

"Nancy Sorenson, attorney. The phone number's on that paper I gave you. I'm her secretary." She got into her car and turned the key in the ignition. The motor sputtered and died. Billie muttered under her breath, rolled down the window, and said as she turned the key again, "Anybody calls about my ad for a roomer, tell them to call back between five-thirty and six-thirty, like it says."

"Yes ma'am."

He watched as she backed down the drive with the motor of her car coughing and bucking, and waved good-bye. Then he went inside, had a bowl of cereal, cleaned up the kitchen, made his bed and Billie's, and wiped both bathrooms clean. It was a good feeling to be in charge of this pretty house with the silent air-conditioning. He watched talk shows and game shows on television, and read another book from his room. His room now, not the girls' room. He made a sandwich for his lunch. The long afternoon stretched before him.

He walked to the end of the street, where Billie had taken him yesterday. The sun, high in the blue sky, made him sweat under his clothes. Not a soul was in sight. For a long time he stood there, peering through his glasses at the white house behind the bushes on the other side, scanning the area of wilderness beside it, catching the distant shine of the lake. Then, with a quick glance around him, he ran across the dry dirt road.

Tall grass enveloped his high-top shoes. Spanish moss hung like cobwebs from the trees. Twigs and grass burrs clung to his T-shirt and jeans. He was Indiana Jones in dense jungle, good-looking and daring and brave, killing snakes and villains and wild animals as he hacked a path to the ruined temple, where dragons guarded the bloodred ruby that would save the world.

A karate chop knocked down a terrorist, and a butt of the head sent another one hurtling into a ravine. A kick tossed a tiger in the air; his band of snarling brothers turned and fled. A mighty punch sent the chief dragon reeling backward into quicksand as the others came rushing forward—

A dog barked, so close that Jim jumped right out of his fantasy. Caught up in his imagination, he'd moved in the wrong direction, closer to the white frame house and in view of it. There was a porch on the back, and on the steps stood an old man wearing khaki pants and a white T-shirt, his face hidden under the brim of a straw hat.

A little black dog dashed across the grass toward Jim, barking furiously. Behind the noise the old man called, "Here girl, here Trudie." The dog kept running and barking. Jim fled, crashing through the undergrowth as if a pride of lions was after him. The barking stopped. Either the old man managed to call off his pet, or the dog lost sight and scent of her prey. Jim kept running until he circled back to the road.

His shoes were soaking wet, and there were burrs all over his jeans. He picked them off as he walked down Orange Blossom Lane, which stretched deserted under the bright June sun. He felt elated. The adventure had broken the monotony of the long and empty day. Now he could go home and think of all sorts of things to do for Billie before she came home from work.

Every night he'd have the table set, and water boiling for her coffee. Grandma had never let him cook, in case, she said, he ruined the food, but he'd learn to cook and have supper waiting every night. He'd do everything he could to please Billie, so that she'd love him as much as she loved her own kids, who, he'd decided, were lazy and spoiled rotten. Before the summer was over he was going to make himself indispensable. Billie wouldn't even remember she was supposed to send him back to Tampa.

But he was going to disobey her too. His adventure had ended too soon. He'd caught a glimpse of the lake, and the dark woods growing around it. The shining water reflected the trees and the white clouds in the blue sky, like an upside-down picture. He wanted to see it again. He was going back, just one more time.

# CHAPTER 4

Billie had said she'd be home by 5:30. At 5:15 the doorbell rang. Jim moved quietly behind the vertical blinds at the living room window. From there he could see the front doorstep without being seen himself.

A man stood in front of the door, younger than Billie, with blond hair, in khaki work clothes. He looked down at his feet and back up while he waited for the door to be opened, then rang the bell again. Behind him, in the drive, Jim saw a navy blue pickup truck in need of a paint job. The man rang the doorbell a third time while Jim stood silently, almost holding his breath. The man walked back to his truck and backed out of the driveway. But he didn't leave. He parked at the curb, in front of the house, and sat there with the window of his truck rolled down.

Jim stayed behind the blinds. It seemed a long time before Billie's car came down the street. The man in the truck followed her into her driveway. She stopped with a screech of brakes in the carport. Jim heard the slam of both car doors as he ran through the dining area into the kitchen. Billie's key grated in the lock of the back door; she held it slightly open as she stood in the carport.

"I came about the room," the young man said.

"The ad said a woman and that's what it means," Billie said sharply. "Can't you read?"

"Here's the money, fifty dollars a week, in advance."

"I'm not taking a man boarder."

"Cash. I have it right here."

"N-O, no. Are you deaf?" She came into the house and closed and locked the door. "Some people," she said.

"I have references," the man called through the door.

Jim remembered that he'd forgotten to start the water for Billie's coffee. He poured it, and placed the mug in the microwave oven, while she took off her shoes.

"I'll give you my boss's phone number," the man called. "Call him and ask him about me." A slip of white paper emerged under the door. Billie picked it up and threw it in the trash can under the sink. They heard the man's footsteps recede, and then the motor of his truck as he started it and drove away.

"I don't know how he got my address," Billie said. "I didn't put it in the ad."

"I guess I gave it to him," Jim admitted. "There

was a man called a little while ago, asked where the room was, I told him. I'm real sorry."

"Okay. Just don't do it again. Don't ever give out your address over the phone." She untucked her blouse and put on an apron. "You have any other calls on the room?" she asked as she rummaged in a kitchen cupboard.

The microwave beeped. Jim handed her the mug of coffee. Again she looked startled. Those lazy kids of hers must never have made her a cup of coffee in their lives.

He said that there'd been two calls just before she came home. He'd told the callers to call back after 5:30, and they did, while Billie was slicing hot dogs into a dish of beans to heat for their supper. Jim took over while she went to the telephone at the far end of the kitchen counter. The first caller was a tourist there for a week and the second wanted to pay at the end of the month. Billie said no to both of them.

There was another call while they were eating their dinner. "That's right," Billie said into the phone. "Fifty dollars a week, share the bath and the kitchen. No, the bus don't come this far. Mm-hm, okay." She hung up and shrugged her shoulders. "I'm too far out of town," she said. "They need a car."

She asked him what he'd done all day, and he said he'd read, watched TV, and walked down the street and back.

"There's a boy your age lives down at the end," Billie said. "Buddy Wellin, he cuts my grass. Maybe you can get to meet him."

"Yes ma'am."

"His parents both work. I don't want you in his house, and I don't want him in here. Most of the parents around here work. It's a working neighborhood. They get to a certain level, they sell, buy something bigger. That's what we were going to do."

"It's real nice here."

"It sure is," Billie said. "That's why I'm working two jobs and taking in a boarder, trying to hold on to my house."

She got up and put their dishes in the sink, moving fast, banging them down hard. Jim washed them while she changed her clothes. Now that he knew how hard she was struggling to keep her house, he'd try to do even more. There was another phone call; Billie came out in her white blouse and black skirt to take it.

"Look, lady, it says adults and that's what it means," she said before she hung up. She looked at Jim. "Has a little boy, says they can sleep in that one little bed," she said. "That's for the birds." He was silent. "I guess you think I'm real hard," Billie said.

"No ma'am."

"When you've been hurt once, you learn to protect yourself. Right after I was divorced, I met a woman got me to invest in a real estate deal. I didn't have a job then, it sounded real good. I was going to make a lot of money and end up vice-president of the company. Anyway I took out a second mortgage on my house, gave her the money, that's the last I ever saw her. My payments went from seven hundred to twelve hundred a month."

"That's a lot of money."

"It sure is," Billie said. "I ever have a real emergency, I'm down the drain. That's why I can't keep you. I'm sorry, but that's the way it is."

She went back to her room to finish dressing.

# CHAPTER 5

**T**he next afternoon Jim went slogging through the jungle again. He emerged from the trees into a marshy area reaching into the lake. Water seeped through the fabric of his high-tops. His feet sank into black ooze.

The lake spread out before him, its surface as smooth as glass in the shimmering heat of the afternoon. Around it, the massed trees looked black. Here and there a patch of roof or strip of white sand beach marked the places where people lived. In the distance, where the lake made its curve, he saw the frameworks of brand-new houses, like wooden skeletons, in a clearing where the trees had been chopped down.

Once, Indians crept through these trees and launched their canoes upon the great gray water. He was Swift Panther, brave of the Tomahawk tribe, handsome and strong, stalking the wicked white men who were trying to take his land. He felt a shad-

26

ow on his foot, looked down and saw a thin black water snake glide across his shoe toward the deeper water of the lake. He recognized it from the chapter on reptiles in fourth grade science. Water snakes were harmless, but his imagination painted the thicker body and heart-shaped head of the poisonous water moccasin. Swift Panther bent down and strangled the deadly reptile with his bare hands, while the black snake swam away with its head out of the water.

The Indian brave lifted his feet out of the ooze and squelched onto firmer ground. The chief, his father, had died, and now Swift Panther must don the feathered headdress. He danced around the pine tree totem pole, intercepted a spy for the troop of soldiers sworn to kill him, and led his braves to victory, all on his way back to the road.

He came out of the bushes not far from Mr. Morrison's solitary mailbox. The old man stood beside it, holding letters in his hand. The little black dog at his heels growled at the sight of Jim.

"Quiet, Trudie," the old man said. He raised his voice. "Come here, boy," he called.

Jim hesitated, then, with one eye on the dog, made his way slowly down the dry dirt road until he stood a few feet from the mailbox. The dog continued to growl, as a reminder that she was still on guard. Up close, Mr. Morrison seemed even older. In the shade of his straw hat, his face was deeply wrinkled. Behind his heavy-rimmed glasses, his eyes were the color of old blue jeans. He was not quite as tall as Jim, in khaki pants and a white T-shirt.

"Can you read, boy?" he asked. His voice was old too.

"Yes sir." Jim kept his distance, to have a head start in case the little growling dog attacked.

"I have cataracts," the old man said. "What does this say?" He held out an envelope from the two or three in his hand. Jim stepped forward, one eye on the dog. "Trudie won't hurt you 'less you hurt me," her master assured him. "Good girl, Trudie, now hush up."

The growling died away, and the little dog dropped her short black tail. Jim looked down at the printed envelope in his hand. "Merchandise Pickup Notice," he read aloud. "Consigned to Mr. H. B. Morrison—"

"That's me. Herbert Benjamin Morrison, only everybody called me Ben long as I can remember. You can call me Ben. What's your name, boy?"

"Jim Allengood, sir. Pleased to meet you." They shook hands, and Jim continued reading. "Thirty-two forty Paradise Lane—"

"Used to be RFD Two," Ben Morrison said. "Then they started building houses and give us all numbers."

"—Orlando, Florida, three-two-eight-four-oh," Jim concluded. "Looks like you have a package to pick up, sir." He examined the paper in his hands. There was no envelope, just a sheet of paper folded and addressed. Inside were pictures of a set of luggage, a clock, a cordless telephone, and a barbecue grill. He read the black print. "It's from Happy Acres, near St. Augustine. Map shows you how to get there. If you go look at their houses, they'll give you one of these prizes."

"It's just a come-on," Ben Morrison said. "They won't give you no such thing." He took the paper from Jim and crumpled the colored pictures. "This is my 'lectric bill." He held out a long green envelope printed in darker green. "How much I owe?"

"Seventy-four dollars and twenty-one cents," Jim said after he scrutinized the bill.

"Daylight robbery," the old man muttered. "What's this one?"

It was an envelope full of discount coupons.

"You take 'em to the store, they give you something off," Jim explained. His grandma and Aunt Bessie had a drawer full of them. "Like this one from the Pizza Palace. You get two dollars off any medium or large pizza."

"You want 'em?" Ben offered. "I don't believe in that stuff."

"Thank you, sir." He stuffed the coupons into the pocket of his jeans.

"Where you live?" Ben asked.

Jim pointed down the street. "Down there. Orange Blossom Lane. I live with my aunt Billie." She was related, even if she wasn't his aunt.

"That's Buzzard Run," Ben said. "Been called that

as long as I lived in this county, near to eighty year. I seen you over here yesterday, didn't I? I can't see to read, but I'm not blind, I seen you coming up from the lake. You want to be careful down there."

"A water moccasin ran right over my foot," Jim boasted.

"Plenty of them in that lake, I shouldn't wonder," Ben said. "Plenty of bass too. I used to go out there in my boat, caught one once weighed thirteen pound. Don't have my boat anymore. Fish from my dock, but it's too hot in the summer. You want to see my boat dock?"

He walked away from Jim, down the sandy narrow path that was his driveway, with his little dog trotting at his heels. "Come on, boy," he called.

Jim followed him. Ben walked slowly, with his shoulders stooped. Trailing him through the heat, Jim remembered the warnings of Grandma and Aunt Bessie when he lived in Tampa, that there were bad people in the world who'd try to entice him into their homes and cars. But he could run and Ben couldn't, and he didn't intend to go inside the house. And so he followed, his wet shoes glopping behind Ben's silent sneakers.

There was a carport on the side of the small frame house, although there was no car under it now, nor anything else. In the back, a flight of four steps led up to the porch. An air conditioner grew out of the window, like those Aunt Bessie had. Ben walked past the house and down the short lawn, toward the lake.

A narrow strip of sand formed a beach between the grass and the water. On one side, a dock stretched out on wooden legs.

"I don't let the kids around here come on my dock," Ben said as they walked along. "They fall in the lake, get drowned, how'd you think I'd feel? You only come down with me, hear?"

"Yes sir."

The little black dog ran ahead of her master to the end of the dock and stood there, pointing her black nose into whatever breeze she sensed in the hot still air. Ben followed, and rested his hand on the last of a series of dock posts. Jim stood beside him. The wood of the dock was gray and brittle. Under the surface of the water he could see a forest of wavy weeds.

"That's where the bass hide," Ben said. "Big 'uns don't come in this close though."

Jim stared out over the glassy gray water. "I sure would love to see a gator," he said.

"They're out there," the old man confirmed. "I keep Trudie away from the water. Gators love dogs. Think they're T-bone steak."

"You ever see one?" Jim asked.

"I built this house, fifty year back, I seen 'em every day. Never seen anything so ugly in my life! I bet even their mothers can't stand the sight of 'em."

"It's real bad to be ugly," Jim said. He blinked as the sun hit his glasses. Indian braves didn't wear glasses. "I guess I better go," he said.

Trudie began to growl, a soft sound in her throat that grew louder. She stood on the dock between Jim and Ben, her nose pointing into the lake and her tail straight out.

"Wait, boy." Ben spoke softly. His hands were big, and stained with large brown splotches. He fastened one of them on Jim's arm, and with the other pointed into the lake. "Trudie sees something out there, don't you, girl? What do you see, Trudie? You see it, boy? Is it a gator?"

Excitement made Jim tense as he scoured the surface of the lake for the huge beast with gaping jaws. There was nothing but the shimmer of heat rising in the still air.

"I don't see a thing," he said in disappointment while Trudie barked across the water.

"Trudie sees him, don't you, girl? Look where she's looking. All you'll see is its eyes, like little bumps."

Jim squinted in the direction of the little dog's nose. Then he saw the cause of her alarm: not a gape-jawed monster but two small dark humps breaking the lake's shiny surface a few yards from the dock. He drew in his breath.

"I think I see it," he breathed.

"It sees us," Ben said softly. "It's hoping we'll be fool enough to go in the water. Some folks feed 'em marshmallows, would you believe it?"

"Marshmallows?" Jim queried. "They eat marshmallows?"

"They say that's what they like. Durn fools. You get 'em used to eating 'em, then one day you don't have any, they take your arm off."

They stood side by side, staring at the pair of humps, which never moved, while Trudie, between them, kept up her barking. Ben turned his head to peer at Jim. "You're not thinking of feeding it, are you, boy?"

"No sir." Jim continued to gaze across the water at the alligator.

"'Cause if you do, you'll never come on my property again. That's the stupidest thing I ever heard, feeding gators."

"Yes sir, sure is."

His eyes were focused on the gator; everything else in the world fell back. Swift Panther swam like a fish, under the scaly body and up on the other side, leaped astride the gator's back, and rode it down down down into depths never before plumbed by any human being—

The humps vanished under the water; there wasn't even a ripple.

"It's gone," Jim said. The tension he'd felt left his body in a sigh, but he was still excited as he stared at the place where the gator had been. "I sure do thank you, sir," he said. "I never seen a gator before, except on TV and in the movies."

"It'll be back. You stay out that lake, hear?"

"Yes sir."

Ben led the way up the slope of the lawn, with

Trudie running ahead of him. "Me and Trudie are going to take a nap," he said. "Every day we lay down after the mailman comes, don't we, girl?"

The little dog wagged her tail as she waited for them at the foot of the porch steps.

"She's cute," Jim said. He bent down and, cautiously at first, rubbed her rough black hair. Her tail wagged faster.

"I don't know what I'd do without Trudie," Ben said. "You come on back, Jim, you hear? I'll look for you when I go out for the mail."

"Yes sir."

Jim walked home fast, wishing it were time for Billie to come home so that he could tell her about the gator.

# CHAPTER 6

The man in the truck was waiting when Billie drove in that evening. Again he parked on the street and followed her into the drive. Again Billie opened the back door as she stood in the carport talking to him. Again Jim listened.

"You didn't call my boss," the man said. "Here's his phone number again. He'll tell you I'm okay."

"I told you I'm not taking a man," Billie said. She came into the house and kicked off her shoes. Jim handed her a mug of coffee. "Get lost," she muttered as the man continued to call through the door.

"I just want a place near my work," he pleaded. "I have a job, Southside Garage. Call that number, they'll tell you."

"Anybody call about the room?" Billie asked.

Jim shook his head. Nobody had called, and there was only one call that evening, after the man went away, before Billie left for her second job. "Sounds like she's on drugs, or crazy," Billie said after she hung up.

"What happens if you don't rent it?" Jim asked.

35

"I can't make it without the rent money. The ad has another day to run, maybe somebody'll call tomorrow. If not I'll have to put it in again."

She sounded tired and pessimistic. It was no time to tell her that he'd disobeyed her and gone to the lake.

The next day he waited for the mailman to come, took Billie's mail inside, and sprinted down the street, arriving at Ben's mailbox just as the mailman placed two envelopes inside it. Ben came down the drive, with Trudie trotting beside him. She wagged her tail as Jim bent down to pat her. He straightened up and read aloud Ben's water bill and a letter asking for money to find missing children.

"Maybe I'll send 'em five dollars," Ben said. Trudie stood between them, wagging her tail, as if they were equal owners. "Thank you, Jim," Ben continued. "That sure is a help. My daughter's taking me to the eye doctor in September, have my cataracts operated on. She lives in South Carolina, that's the earliest she can make it."

"How do you get groceries and stuff?"

"Miz Gruber down the street takes me to the grocery store, anyplace else I have to go."

They said good-bye. Jim crossed the road as if he were going home. Then, when Ben and Trudie were out of sight around the corner of the house, he crossed it again and slipped into the trees. For a little while he played Swift Panther. But it was make-believe now, a kids' game. There was something much better waiting for him. He curbed his impatience until he felt that Ben and Trudie would have fallen asleep, then sneaked through the undergrowth onto Ben's lawn and out to the end of the dock.

His heart leaped as he scanned the surface of the lake. A few yards out, in the same place as yesterday, the alligator's eyebrows made a double hump on the surface of the shiny gray water. He sat down on the end of the dock with his legs dangling.

"Hi, Gator," he called. "Did you come back to see me? You sure are ugly, you know that? Me too, Gator. I guess we're two of a kind."

He sat there for a long time, until the humps submerged. Then he walked home, reviewing in his mind all that he knew about alligators, and hugging his secret.

The man in the pickup truck didn't come that evening, and there were no calls for the room. Billie was tired and short-tempered. Jim washed their supper dishes while she changed her clothes. She came into the kitchen dressed for work, went to the telephone, and dialed a number from a piece of paper in her hand. It looked like the piece of paper given to her by the man in the pickup truck. Jim was shocked. He thought she'd thrown it away.

She asked for Mr. Tom Edelbert. "This is Billie Newhouse," she said brusquely. "Does a Troy Markham work for you?"

Jim stopped washing dishes and listened to her side of the conversation. Between pauses she asked:

"How long?" . . . "What's he like?" . . . "Does he drink or do drugs?" . . . Finally she said, "Thank you," and hung up.

"You going to rent your room to that guy, Billie?" Jim asked in a tone of voice that conveyed what a crazy idea it was.

"You have a better idea?" she snapped.

The next afternoon he went to read Ben's mail, and again waited for Ben and Trudie to fall asleep before sneaking onto the dock. The alligator was waiting for him. Ben had given Jim another discount coupon. Jim folded it into a paper airplane and launched it across the water. It dived when it should have soared, and floated back toward the beach. The alligator didn't stir.

The navy blue pickup truck arrived at the curb fifteen minutes before Billie came home and followed her car into the drive. She stood at the door to talk. Jim couldn't see the young man in khaki work clothes, but he could hear his voice.

"Mr. Edelbert told me you called him," he said. "That mean you're going to let me have the room?"

"Not so fast," Billie snapped. "I'm a single parent, I have rules."

"I'll just be here to sleep, ma'am, won't set foot outside my room 'less you invite me."

"Where you living now?"

"I'm bunking with a friend on the other side of town. I need to be near my work."

"How come you have a job, you don't have your own place?"

"I did have, but I ran up a lot of debt on my credit cards. My car was repossessed, I moved in with my folks. Then I totaled my stepfather's car one night, he threw me out. We never did get along."

"You sound like a real winner," Billie said.

"I messed up real bad, but I learned my lesson."

"Where'd you get that truck?"

"My boss lets me use it. He wants to be sure I get to work. I'm the only one he has can work on sports cars. I can take 'em apart, put 'em back together again, like you wouldn't believe. I'm going into business for myself when I get some money."

"Oh sure." She stared at him for what seemed a long time. Finally she said, "The room's just till August. My girls get back from their father, I'll find a woman renter, I want you out."

"That's okay. I plan to rent a little studio apartment soon as I save some money."

"No smoking or drinking in the house, and don't bring your girlfriends here."

"No problem."

"You have to share the bathroom."

"That's fine." There was a pause. "You didn't find anyone else to take it," the young man pointed out. "A lot of people would think it was out in the boonies."

"A lot of people can go jump in the lake."

"I'm at work all day, some nights too, and I eat out. I won't be any bother to you, and I have the rent right here."

Jim knew then that Billie would give in. She needed the money.

"You want to look at the room?" she asked.

"It'll be fine. If it's okay with you, I'll move right in. I have my stuff in the truck."

Billie stood drinking her coffee while Troy Markham carried in his belongings in a variety of tote bags and a cardboard box. He had blue eyes and broad shoulders. Jim hated him. He didn't want somebody else to make Billie's life easier, with his fifty dollars a week. He wanted to do that himself, to make himself so useful that Billie couldn't do without him.

In a few minutes Troy Markham had moved in. After he roared off in his truck to have his supper, Billie picked up the telephone. "I'm going to call the Pizza Palace, order a pizza. I don't have time to cook. I'll tell them what I want, you run down and get it, okay? What do you like on pizza?"

"Anything except anchovies."

She ordered a medium sausage-and-onion pizza, and handed Jim one of the twenty-dollar bills her new roomer had given her as part of his rent. "A medium's big enough," she said. "I can't eat more'n a couple pieces."

She told him where it was, down to the main road and turn right, along to the little shopping center.

When he got back she was dressed for work in her black skirt and white blouse.

"This is too much," she said when he gave her the change.

"I had a coupon, two dollars off on a medium pizza."

"That was real smart," Billie said. "Here, you take the two dollars."

He reared away from the table, set with two plates and the pizza box between them. "It's to help out," he said.

"We'll split it, a dollar for you and a dollar for me." She laid the dollar bill beside his plate. "Go on, take it. You have to have some money in your pocket."

"Aunt Bessie gave me a dollar. I still have it."

"This one'll keep it company."

He wouldn't take it. Troy Markham wasn't the only one who could make a contribution. They had just finished eating when the telephone rang. Billie got up to answer it, and Jim began to clear the table.

"It's rented," he heard Billie say. "I sure am sorry, but there's nothing I can do. Damn," she said as she hung up the phone. "There's a lady sounds real nice, has her own car, said she'd love to have the room. Wouldn't you know it?"

"Call her back," Jim cried. "Give that guy his money back!"

"I didn't get her number," Billie said. "Anyway, a deal's a deal." She glanced at her watch and picked her car keys out of her bag.

41

"I don't like him," Jim said.

"There's all kinds of people you won't like and have to get along with. That's life." She was at the door, ready to go. "Listen, if he steps out of line, he's out of here. He so much as looks the wrong way at you, you let me know, okay?"

"Yes ma'am," Jim said sullenly.

His world had had just the right number of people in it until Troy Markham came along. Now there was one too many.

# CHAPTER 7

He could hardly wait for Billie to come out from her room the next morning.

"He sat down watched TV with me without I asked him!" he cried as he thrust a mug of coffee at her. "He looked in my room! Right now he's in the shower using up all the hot water!"

"I'm running late," Billie said, and left, carrying her coffee.

Five minutes later Troy Markham came out, whistling, with his blond hair wet from the shower.

"Morning, Jim," he said cheerfully. "Miz Newhouse leave, did she?"

Jim stuffed his mouth full of cereal.

"Guess I'll be on my way," Troy said.

He'd parked his truck on the grass beside the drive, so as not to block Billie. Jim heard the motor start. The sound of it died away, but the thought of Troy Markham's presence in the household ruined his whole day. He told his alligator about it that afternoon as he dangled his legs over the water with his eyes fixed on the humps.

"I'd sooner you moved in than him," he said. In spite of himself, he laughed at the idea. "Hey, wouldn't that be something? You think you could fit in the other bed in my room, Gator?"

There was no answer, not even a ripple when his friend submerged. Jim wondered what it saw from a few yards out. Could it see him on the dock, with his legs hanging down? Could it hear him? The fourth grade science book said that alligators had poor eyesight and hearing. They moved fast on land, though, at least for the first half mile, up to thirty miles an hour.

Troy Markham got home before Billie that evening. He went to his room in his work clothes, took a shower, and came out in clean jeans and a shirt.

"I'm going get me some supper, see a movie," he said. "You want to come along?"

"I'm waiting on my aunt," Jim said coldly, and refocused his attention on the television set. He was watching "M*A*S*H."

Troy stood behind the couch in the TV room. "Sure is funny," he said. "You play any sports, Jim?"

"No."

Troy left. As soon as Jim heard the rough beat of Billie's motor coming down the street he turned off the television set and put a mug of water in the microwave oven. She was hardly inside the door before he pounced on her.

"He took another shower, that's two in one day! And he wanted me to go to supper and the movies with him, and he asked did I play sports!"

Billie sighed. There were dark circles under her eyes. "Look," she said, "it's Friday, I had a real rough week, and I have a long night coming up. Don't bother me unless it's something real bad, okay? Tomorrow and Sunday I'll sleep in, won't be so tired." She added as she went toward her room with her shoes in her hand, "Playing sports might not be a bad idea. You don't want to sit around the house so much."

He didn't sit around the house, he went every day to Ben's dock to see his gator. If he'd told her that the first day, it might have been okay, but if he told her now, in her present frame of mind, he'd be in trouble.

When she came to cook their dinner he said, "I been going down to Mr. Morrison's to read his mail. He told me to call him Ben."

"I guess that's okay," Billie said. "Just don't bother him, hear? You take that hamburger out the freezer like I told you?"

He'd been so absorbed in thoughts of Troy Markham that he'd forgotten. Billie was angry. She threw the frozen slab of hamburger meat into the microwave oven.

"Now I have to stand around waiting for it to defrost," she cried. "You better mind me when I tell you to do something!"

She didn't say that if he didn't, sh
back to Tampa, but in his mind he hea
Everything had gone bad, and it
Markham's fault.

# CHAPTER 8

On Saturday morning Troy got up and went to work. Billie slept until ten o'clock; she told Jim that it was after midnight when she got home.

"Saturdays I go to the bank, buy groceries, run by the Laundromat," she said. "My washer broke down, I can't afford another repair bill right now."

Jim went with her to the bank and the supermarket, and helped to put the food away. Then they collected the dirty clothes and towels and sheets, and Billie drove to the Laundromat in the strip of shops around the corner.

"We'll go get something t'eat while they're washing," she said. "You want to go to McDonald's?"

"I have two coupons for Wendy's."

"You and your coupons," she said, and drove to Wendy's. They sat at a table in the window. Jim finished first.

"You want another hamburger?" Billie asked. "We saved enough on your coupons to get you another one."

"I'm full." He would have loved another, but he

wanted to show her that Troy Markham wasn't the only one who could help with expenses. He sat watching her. Her hair was pulled back, and she wore no makeup. But she was still pretty. "Billie?" he asked.

She looked at him with her steady brown eyes. "What?"

"How come you got a divorce?"

"My husband found himself a little teenybopper. That answer your question?"

"Yes ma'am. I'm sorry."

"That's okay. I got over it. At least he pays the child support, keeps in touch with the girls."

"Why'd you let them go to him?"

"He wanted to have them, they wanted to go. He has a wife home all day with a new baby. And he belongs to a club with a pool and tennis courts. It's better than sitting around my house all day."

"What if . . . ," Jim began. He cleared his throat. "If they wanted to live with him, would you let them?"

"Over my dead body! Well, if they wanted to, I guess I'd have to. But I don't know what I'd do without my girls."

"Yes ma'am," he said, and sighed inwardly. If he was going to become a permanent boarder he'd have to learn to get along with those spoiled-rotten girls.

They went back to the Laundromat and put the damp clothes into a laundry basket. Billie remembered that she'd forgotten to buy hot dog buns with her groceries. She handed Jim a dollar bill.

"Run to the 7-Eleven, get a pack of hot dog buns while I put the clothes in the car," she said.

He passed the candy section on his way to the shelf with the buns. His eyes lingered on the chocolate bars, bubble gum, licorice, marshmallows—big bags of fat white marshmallows, seventy-nine cents. He picked up one of them. At the counter he bought the hot dog buns out of Billie's dollar and the marshmallows out of his own dollar, and asked for them to be put in separate bags.

"What's that?" Billie asked, pointing to the bag he kept.

"I bought some candy."

"Be sure you clean your teeth after you eat it."

In his mind he saw the alligator brushing away with a giant toothbrush. He managed not to smile as he said, "Yes ma'am."

Back at the house, she hung out the clothes they'd washed. There was a dryer in the storeroom, beside the broken washing machine, but she only used it when the weather was bad. There were two girls' bikes in there too.

"Maybe you can ride Jennifer's," Billie said. "I'll ask her when I call them tomorrow."

"Thank you ma'am. I don't like riding girls' bikes."

"Suit yourself." She looked at her watch. "I can't

believe it, it's only two o'clock. I was going to clean the bathrooms but you're keeping them up so nice I don't have to. I guess I'll iron a few clothes 'fore I go to work."

"I can iron."

"You're a good kid, but you don't have to work every single minute," Billie said. "I'll do the ironing, you do something for fun."

"I could go down help Mr. Morrison read his mail."

"That would be real nice."

He hesitated. "Billie," he said, "would it be okay I ask him to pay me for it?"

"We don't need money that bad, Jim," she said. "Do it because he's your friend."

He was elated as he hurried down the street with his bag of marshmallows in the paper bag. Billie had said, "We don't need money that bad." We. She was including him in the family. And she'd referred to Ben as his friend. He'd been here a week and he had a friend, two friends counting his gator, three, because Trudie was like his own dog now, trotting to meet him every afternoon, licking his hand.

Not this afternoon, though. He'd known that Ben would have collected his mail half an hour ago and gone to take his nap. The little house was quiet; the lake shone under the glaring sun. Excitement rose inside him as he surveyed it from the end of the dock. A few yards out, the dark double hump marked his friend's presence.

He called softly across the water. "Hey, Gator, I brought you some dessert! You like marshmallows?"

He tore open the plastic bag with his teeth. The candies felt soft and warm in his hand. One by one he flung them on the water. They floated away from him, bobbing in the direction of those two dark humps. He used up half the bag. The humps didn't move.

Disappointed, he called, "I'm not going to give you any more." And then he tensed. The water parted. Jaws fanged with long white teeth slashed the air and sucked in mouthfuls of marshmallow-laden water as the reptile's hidden body moved rapidly after the bobbing candies. Then, sinking beneath the water as fast as it had risen from it, the creature was gone. Only a ripple marked the spot where it disappeared.

Exhilaration made Jim leap in the air. He'd made contact! He'd shown the gator that it had a friend who didn't hate its ugliness, who'd be kind to it and feed it marshmallows. He still had half a bag left.

He walked home. There was singing in his ears, as if his whole body were rejoicing. It had been a good day.

# CHAPTER 9

His good mood vanished as he came within sight of Billie's house. Troy Markham was up on a ladder, nailing a basketball hoop onto the front of the carport.

"Did my aunt say you could do that?" Jim demanded.

"Sure did," Troy said cheerfully. "You want to shoot some baskets?"

"No." Jim went into the house and hid the remaining marshmallows in a cupboard. Billie was folding up the ironing board. He took it from her and put it away in the closet where she kept cleaning supplies.

"You see what Troy's doing?" she asked.

"I hate basketball!" What he really hated was the approval in her voice when she spoke of the roomer.

"You need some exercise. You sit around the house too much." She looked at her watch. "I still have some time before I get dressed," she said. "I'm going to write Aunt Bessie, tell her you're doing real good. You write her too, I'll put it in with mine."

Unwillingly, Jim sat down with her at the table in the dining area and accepted a sheet of writing paper. He didn't want to write to Aunt Bessie, or even think of her; he wanted to pretend that she didn't exist. His grandma had died and left him; pretty soon Aunt Bessie would die too. That part of his life was over.

Troy Markham came into the kitchen and washed his hands at the sink. "I put your hammer back in the storeroom," he said. "I see you have a lawn mower in there. Jim cut your grass?"

"It's not working," Billie said. "I can't afford to keep getting it repaired."

"I'll take a look at it."

They heard the sound of the lawn mower out in the carport, the pull of the cable followed by the sputter of the motor that died and gurgled and died again. Troy repeated the process several times before he came inside.

"All that's wrong with it is it needs new spark plugs," he said. "I can fix it, you want me to."

"I have a boy cut the grass," Billie said. "It's cheaper than keep repairing that thing." She frowned. "He was supposed to come yesterday. I'll have to get after him."

"He fixes the lawn mower, I could cut your grass," Jim said. "I could cut other people's too, make some money."

"It's just another motor to keep up. I have all I can handle right now."

"I can buy the spark plugs for around ten dollars," Troy said. "Have it fixed in no time."

"Let him, Billie," Jim begged.

She shrugged and handed Troy a twenty-dollar bill from her bag. "If it breaks down again, that's it," she warned.

"You want to come with me, Jim?" Troy asked.

"No."

"No thank you, sir," Billie said.

"No thank you, sir."

"Even if you don't like people you still have to be polite," Billie instructed him after Troy left to buy the spark plugs. "He's doing you a favor. Why don't you like him?"

Because he wanted to be able to do for her the things Troy did, so that she wouldn't need Troy, wouldn't need anybody but him. If he said that, she'd think he was trying to take over. People didn't like that. He said nothing.

"You think I'm going to like him better'n you because he's good-looking?" Billie asked. "He's a roomer, is all. When my girls come back, out he goes." He wished she wouldn't talk about her girls coming back.

They finished their letters. Jim's was very short. Billie addressed the envelope and licked the flap. When she looked up at him, she had the expression of someone who'd made a hard decision.

"You're a good kid, Jim," she said. "I like having you here. But I can't keep you past the summer. I asked Aunt Bessie if she found your daddy's family yet. They'll be real glad to know where you are."

She knew as well as he did that if they wanted to know where he was, they could have found out years ago.

"You were the only child," Billie said. "Your mama and daddy died in a fire trying to save you. You know that, don't you?"

"Yes ma'am." Grandma had told him, over and over, as if it were a story in a book. The fire broke out after supper, on a summer evening. He was a baby, asleep in his crib upstairs. His mama and daddy were painting the back porch. By the time they smelled smoke, the staircase was ablaze.

His daddy yelled to his mama to call the fire department, and charged upstairs to get the baby. She made the call and went after him. When the firemen came they found the two bodies at the top of the stairs. They broke a window to get into the baby's room, where the little boy was still fast asleep. That was why he had no photos of his family; they were burned up in the fire.

"All your mama and daddy thought about was getting you out of there," Billie said. "But the fire started under the stairs and the smoke was real bad, that's what killed them. They sure did love you. They say there were a hundred people at their funeral."

When Grandma told the story, it made him feel proud, with tears in his eyes. But Billie told it to make him feel good about going back to Georgia, as if the relatives who didn't want him then would want him now. The tears in his eyes were from anger, that they didn't want him and that Billie wanted to send him there.

It was a relief when Troy came in, waving a plastic bag from Kmart. In his other hand he held an old gas can Jim had seen in the storeroom. "I took the gas can, bought some gas and oil for the motor," Troy said as he counted change into Billie's hand. "Okay, Jim, let's fix that lawn mower!"

Jim followed him into the carport. If he watched carefully he could do the repair himself the next time. Troy explained each step as he replaced the worn-out spark plugs, then poured gasoline into the motor and added a little oil. It was exhilarating to hear it start when he pulled the cable. Jim almost cheered along with Troy, and ran after him as he wheeled the mower onto the front lawn.

Troy mowed a strip of grass, then Jim took over. He walked behind the clattering machine, up and down, up and down, pacing the small lawn, down the side, across the backyard. When he came back to the carport, Billie was standing with Troy, dressed for work. They clapped their hands and cheered. Jim turned off the motor.

"You can tell that kid you don't need him anymore," he said to Billie. "I'll cut your grass from now on."

"Okay, but don't you have something to say to Troy?" Jim stared at her. "Don't you want to tell him thank you for fixing the mower?"

"Thanks."

"That's okay," Troy said. He looked at Billie. "I'd work on your car, only it wouldn't be worth the price of the parts. You sure do need a new car."

"Gee thanks. I'll stop and pick up a Mercedes tomorrow."

Troy grinned at her sarcasm. "I'll show you how to clean the blades," he said to Jim. "That's real important. Then I guess I better take a shower and go get some supper. You want to come with me?"

"I already ate."

"That was hours ago," Billie said. "All I'm fixing is some canned soup. Go on and eat with him."

"I'm not hungry."

"That little old hamburger's not going to last you all day. I'll give you some money, you can get what you want."

"I don't want to go," Jim said sullenly.

Troy shrugged. "Suit yourself," he said, and went to take a shower.

"Why don't you like him?" Billie demanded. "He fixed the mower for you."

He was pleased that the mower was fixed, but he wished that it wasn't Troy who came to the rescue again. It sounded ungrateful, and so he was silent. He was glad when Troy and then Billie left, and he was alone in the house.

# CHAPTER 10

By the time Billie got up on Sunday, Jim had canvassed Orange Blossom Lane for lawn-mowing jobs.

"I only had one man say I could cut his grass, but two ladies asked me did I baby-sit," he said as she sipped her coffee. "One said I can sit with her kids tonight."

"What's her name?"

"Miz Milligan."

Billie raised her eyes to the ceiling. "Three kids, all monsters. Don't you let them in here!"

"No ma'am." He was elated, could feel the money in his hands and imagine himself handing it to Billie.

"I'll go get dressed, run the vacuum," she said.

"I'll do it!"

"You're a real big help, but you don't need to work all the time."

"I want to do it," he insisted.

He used the vacuum cleaner in every room except Troy Markham's. Then, while Billie spoke to her children over the telephone in the kitchen, he dusted the furniture and eavesdropped on her side of the conversation. Except for a question now and then, she listened more than she talked. After she hung up she said, "They're going swimming at the club and out to dinner."

Jim made a sound to indicate that he was listening.

"They're taking tennis lessons."

"Their daddy must be real rich," Jim said.

"He's a computer whiz. We went into debt so he could start his own business. Right after the divorce, he sold out to one of the big companies, moved to Atlanta to work for them."

"Computers are great."

"Jennifer's real good with them. Up there she can work on her daddy's."

They heard Troy's truck. He'd got up later than usual, but before Billie, and gone out for breakfast. He came in wearing shorts and a T-shirt.

"Man, it's hot out there," he said. "You want to go swimming?" He looked from Billie to Jim.

"I can't swim," Jim said.

"About time you learned."

"I don't have a swimsuit."

"We'll get you one." Troy looked at Billie. "How about it, Miz Newhouse? You have a swimsuit?"

"I can't remember the last time I had it on," she said. "Usually I clean house on Sundays, but Jim did all that." She looked at Jim. "You want to learn to swim?" she asked. "Every kid in Florida should know how to swim."

On the one hand, Jim agreed with her. On the other, he preferred not to take lessons from Troy Markham. But Billie was enthusiastic, and Troy seemed to think that meant that Jim wanted to go too. Within a few minutes they were crammed into the pickup truck, heading for one of the county parks, with a stop at Wal-Mart for a pair of swimming trunks. Jim tried them on in the dressing room, and kept them on, under his jeans, while Billie paid for them.

The park was in a country area, on the shore of a lake with a white sand beach. In spite of himself Jim felt a surge of excitement as Troy pulled into the parking lot. He jumped out of the truck and felt hot asphalt under his bare feet.

"Put your shoes on," Billie called as she followed him with his high-tops and an armful of towels.

Ignoring her, he hopped across the burning surface onto grass set with picnic tables, and then onto the sand, where people sprawled on towels and blankets. A long time ago, when he lived in Tampa, visiting relatives took him to the beach. That was a long beach, on the Gulf of Mexico, stretching away as far as he could see in both directions, with the salty green ocean surging onto it and pulling back. He was maybe seven, a thin ugly kid with red hair, excited by the power of the waves even as they knocked him down.

This beach was a large area of white sand and

green grass between the road and the lake, which was much bigger than Ben's lake. Far out, Jim saw a boat pulling a water-skier, and tiny houses scattered on the opposite shore. The water was gray, ruffled by the breeze that came off it. Kids played in the sand and waded in the water.

Troy raced into the lake and swam away from the beach in long fast strokes, then turned and came back. Dripping wet, in dark red trunks, he came to where Billie had dropped their towels on the sand.

"You coming in?" he asked.

She nodded, and looked at Jim. "How about it, Jim? You ready?"

Jim followed them into waist-deep water. It felt warm against his hot body, and cold around his feet. He was excited, and a little bit nervous. Suppose there were alligators, not as friendly as his own? There wouldn't be, not with all these people, and boats pulling in and out of a ramp farther along the shoreline.

Billie stood on one side of him and Troy on the other. Under their direction, with their hands supporting him, he struggled to relax as he lay facedown upon the water. Troy told him to take a deep breath, then dunk his head and breathe out. It was like blowing bubbles, except that he opened his mouth and came up coughing, with water up his nose.

"You'll swallow a lot of water before you can swim," Billie said. "Try again."

She was right. He must have gulped in gallons of water, a small ocean of water, as he splashed and gurgled and tried to coordinate his breathing.

"Great," Troy said at last. "Now turn over, let's see can you float."

He lay on his back with their hands underneath him and floated like a leaf, until they took away their support. Immediately he sank, and came up with his nose full of water, coughing and thrashing, and blinking without his glasses, which he'd left in the cab of the truck.

"You forgot to breathe," Troy told him.

Jim pointed to a girl much younger than himself who was striking out into the lake with her arms flashing and her head down in the water.

"I want to do that!"

"Okay, but she had to learn to breathe first, and so do you."

He practiced again, then Troy showed him some swimming strokes while Billie went to dry herself. Suddenly she was calling them out of the water because it was time for her to go to work.

"We just got here!" Jim protested.

But he was elated as he ran onto the grass and dried himself on the towel Billie tossed to him. He was learning to swim. He had a lawn-mowing job and a baby-sitting job, and he'd get others. By the end of the summer he'd be making enough money to pay Billie for her spare room. As for Troy, he wasn't too bad when you got to know him, and he'd be moving out at the end of the summer.

"You're doing real well," Troy said as he put the truck in gear and backed out of the parking space, and Billie added, "You'll be a champion swimmer by the time you go back to Tampa."

Why did she have to mention that? Jim's happy mood evaporated as Troy, seizing upon the subject as if there were nothing else in the world to talk about, demanded, "What's this about going back to Tampa?"

Billie explained the situation. Jim wished that he could jump out of the truck, or block his ears. "So I have to take him back when school starts," she ended.

"Looks to me like he's a big help," Troy said.

"He sure is." Billie put her arm around Jim's shoulders. "I don't know what I'd do without him. But I can't afford to keep him."

"Maybe I can help out, once I get on my feet."

"What am I going to do if he gets sick? My kids have health insurance through their daddy, but there's no way I could pay a big medical bill right now. I'm working two jobs already. I can't take on any more."

They drove on in silence. Jim was glad. He hoped the subject was closed forever. Whenever Billie mentioned Tampa he felt afraid, as if he had to go back right now, this very minute, as if he'd be torn away from everything he'd gained in the last week.

He wished, when they got home, that he could tell his alligator how he felt. But it was too late; Ben and Trudie would be up from their nap, and the gator back in its hole. He wondered if it missed him.

# CHAPTER 11

On Monday morning Jim trundled his lawn mower down the street to perform his first lawn-cutting job, wearing his swimming trunks as shorts. He returned home sweating and triumphant. He'd earned ten dollars, and had another eight from baby-sitting. He could pay back Billie for his trunks, buy some more marshmallows, and still have money left over.

By the time he cleaned the blades, took a shower, and had his lunch, it was almost time to go to Ben's. He read while he waited for the mailman to come. He was working his way through the books in his room. Some were too childish, but there were several that dealt with teenage problems. They were all about girls.

It was a world almost as foreign to him as the fantasy jungles inhabited by Indiana Jones and Swift Panther. Girls didn't call boys who looked the way he did. Even if they did, it cost money to go around with other kids. He'd never had any, and whatever he could earn now was reserved for what he'd heard called the cost of living. By the time Troy moved out, he wanted to have enough money to rent the spare room and prove to Billie that he could support himself.

Close to 1:30 he heard the mailman's van. He brought in Billie's mail and walked down the street. The blue sky of the morning had turned gray, and a strong breeze bent the long leaves of the palm trees planted in some of the lawns. Ben was standing beside his mailbox, holding a handful of advertising brochures. Jim stooped down to play with Trudie.

"You really like Trudie, don't you, boy?" Ben asked. "You ever have a dog of your own?"

"A long time ago, when I lived with my grand-ma, she had a dog, but it died. She never did get another one."

"I worry about what will happen to Trudie if any-thing happens to me," Ben said. "Would you take her? Would your aunt let you?"

"Yes sir!" He answered without thinking, full of pride for Ben's confidence in him, and refusing to consider the objections Billie might make. He knew that she liked animals—she patted the neighbor's cat. And even though she said she didn't have pets because she didn't have time to take care of them, she wouldn't have the heart to refuse one whose master just died. That thought brought another. "I don't want you to die," he said.

"I'm not going for a while yet," Ben assured him. "And Trudie might go first, she's thirteen years old.

One time, dogs didn't live any longer'n that. But I feel good knowing if anything happens, you'll take care of her."

Jim gave Trudie a last pat and stood up. "You have anything you want me to read, sir?" he asked.

Ben waved the brochures. "Garbage," he said. "Straight into the trash can."

He turned toward the backyard, with Trudie leading the way. Jim followed them. "Sir," he said, "the kid that cuts your grass, does he do a good job?"

"He don't sweep up after he edges," Ben said. "And he don't come when he's supposed to, comes when he durn well pleases."

"I have my own lawn mower now and I thought, if you're not satisfied with this kid, maybe I could do your yard."

"You have an edger?"

"No sir, but I could do it with a shovel."

"That's okay them little yards, but I have a big yard. Take you all day to edge it with a shovel. You better get you an edger."

"Yes sir."

That was a blow; he hadn't counted on having to buy more equipment. He stood with Ben beside the house, looking across the lake. Wind whipped the surface into choppy white-crested waves. A gray haze obliterated the trees on the other side.

"Rain coming across," Ben said. "I like to stand here, watch it come closer."

A jagged branch of lightning lit the black sky, radiating fire from its forked main artery. The first fat splotches of rain landed on Jim's arms.

"We better get in the house," Ben said.

"Thank you, sir, I'm not allowed in people's houses. I'll run on home. You go take your nap."

He started for home, wondering if his gator realized that they'd have to miss their visit that afternoon. The rain came down thick and fast as he ran across the dirt road onto Orange Blossom Lane. A crack of thunder sounded overhead.

"Hey kid!" The shouted greeting came from the house he was passing. A boy stood under the carport, big and broad-shouldered with a pudgy face, barefoot in shorts and a T-shirt, gesturing for Jim to join him. "Come on out the rain!" he shouted.

Even Swift Panther would take shelter from thunder and lightning. Jim ran up the drive, slowing his pace as he came closer to the boy, standing a few steps away from him under the carport, aware of the racy-looking yellow bicycle leaning against the wall.

"Hi," the boy said, and held out his hand. "Buddy Wellin."

"Jim Allengood."

They shook hands self-consciously.

"You're the kid going to cut the Lopezes' grass," Buddy Wellin said. "They used to be one of my customers." He grinned. "I don't care. I hate mowing lawns."

"Why'd you do it then?"

"My dad makes me. He don't want me sitting around the house all day. I'll tell you who I have, you go tell 'em you'll do their lawns from now on. Then they'll fire me. You going to do Old Man Morrison's? I see you over there talking to him all the time."

"I help him read his mail. He said I have to have an edger."

"He's mean," Buddy Wellin said. "Keeps saying I have to sweep up after I edge. Whose kid are you? Where you live?"

"Twenty-three twenty-four. I live with my aunt, Miz Billie Newhouse." It wasn't necessary to say that he was only there for the summer. By the end of the summer, he'd be permanent.

"You want to come in, have a Coke?"

"Your folks home?"

"They're at work."

"I'm not allowed in anybody's house 'less the parents are home."

"Me neither," Buddy said cheerfully. "But we better not stand out here in case we get struck by lightning. You know Florida's the lightning capital of the world?" Jim didn't bother to answer; everybody knew that. "Let's go in the storeroom," Buddy said.

There were folding lawn chairs stacked in the storage room beside the washer and dryer. Buddy set up two of them a little way back from the open door and brought two Cokes from inside the house. When he opened the back door, Jim could hear rock music playing. The rain was a downpour now, falling in solid sheets, obliterating the houses across the street, even the house next door, hitting the ground and the rooftops with so much noise that they had to raise their voices. Sitting beside Jim, drinking from a can of Coke as they gazed across the carport into the storm, Buddy asked how old he was.

"Thirteen."

"Me too. You'll go to Lakewood High. That's where I go."

"One of my cousins goes there."

"Yeah, I know, Jennifer. She's a pain in the butt, and Lorraine's a brat. All the kids on this street are brats. There's no boys our age, we're the only ones."

"There was only one boy my age where I lived in Tampa."

"Tampa's neat. You can go to the beach."

Jim didn't say that he'd been to the beach only once in all the years he'd lived in Tampa. He said nothing at all about living with Grandma and Aunt Bessie. That part of his life was over. He wasn't going back to it.

It was easy to be silent. Buddy talked without listening, about school, about the people who lived on the street, about his family. He had a brother in the air force and a married sister. His folks thought he was spoiled now that he was the only one left at home.

The rain stopped as suddenly as it had started. The air felt cool, but the sun was already out, beginning to heat up the waterlogged earth.

"You want to go bike riding?" Buddy offered. "I'll show you an orange grove where there's a million dollars buried."

"I don't have a bike. I'm getting one." It wasn't a lie. He would get one, when he was earning enough money.

"You like to go to the movies?"

"I guess."

"You want to go tonight? My dad'll take us and pick us up."

"If it's okay with my aunt."

He asked her the moment she opened the door after she came home from work. She said that he could go, and showed him a key to the back door hidden behind a drainpipe on the side of the house. She showed it to Troy too. Whoever came home first could use it to get into the house.

"Then put it right back," she instructed. "I keep it there in case I lock myself out."

So now he had a buddy. They hung out in each other's carports, and lent each other gasoline for their lawn mowers when one of them ran out. Sometimes Troy took Buddy to buy gasoline and oil, and sometimes Mr. Wellin took Jim. The one thing Jim wouldn't share were his afternoon visits to his alligator. For one thing, Buddy was a blabbermouth; he'd have every kid on the street down there, watching for the humps, tossing marshmallows, until some adult found out what was going on and stopped it. And for another, Jim didn't want to share his gator with anyone. It was his special friend. They had a bond in common.

"What do you do every day down at the old man's?" Buddy asked.

"I do jobs for him," Jim lied.

"I wish he'd let you cut his grass," Buddy grumbled.

"I told you, he said I have to have an edger. That's what everybody says." He'd canvassed Buddy's customers, and other neighbors, with no success.

"My dad won't let me quit my jobs," Buddy said. "And he won't let me lend you our edger. Hey!" His gray eyes lit up. "You know what we could do? We could be partners! You could mow, I could edge! That'd be great!"

"What about your dad?"

"He'll be glad," Buddy said. "He won't have to keep getting the lawn mower repaired. I do five lawns now, ten dollars each. The two of us could do ten, split the money, I'd still make as much."

Fifty dollars a week! Enough to rent Troy's room when he moved out! For once, Jim was as talkative as Buddy as they worked out the details of their partnership. Between them they already had six jobs. He'd go back to the people who'd said he had to have an edger, looking for more customers, as many as he could get. There was no reason he had to stop at ten.

He felt powerful, and superior to Buddy even

though he was two months younger. Buddy was the baby of his family. He'd never had other people depending on him. He spent all his lawn-mowing money on his CD collection and his Nintendo games. He was a big kid.

# CHAPTER 12

Billie agreed to the partnership as long as they took on only ten lawns. Two a day, in the mornings when it was cool, weekends off, she decreed. That was enough for kids their age.

There was a shape now to Jim's days and weeks. Weekdays he and Buddy cut two lawns in the morning. He showered, had lunch, walked down the street to help Ben read his mail, and fed his alligator.

On the way home he stopped at Buddy's. Sometimes they sat in the carport, listening to tapes playing inside the house, and sometimes they shot baskets at Billie's house. After dinner, unless he had a baby-sitting job, he either stayed at home or he and Buddy went to the movies or one of the malls. Sometimes Mr. Wellin provided transportation and sometimes Troy did.

Buddy's father was a big man; everything he said sounded like an order. Mrs. Wellin was short and heavy and nervous, with blond hair. Jim decided that he liked them as long as he didn't spend much time with them.

Every Saturday he helped Billie with the shopping and the laundry, mowed her lawn, and borrowed Buddy's edger to edge it. The Wellins' lawn was one of their regular ten-dollar jobs, but Jim insisted on doing Billie's free, and Buddy didn't argue the point.

Saving Billie ten dollars a week was like giving her that amount. Jim wanted to give her more, but she said that he needed his money for himself. He bought a new pair of high-tops and some underwear out of his first week's pay, and used his baby-sitting money to cover his half of the expenses for gas and oil, and for pocket money. The second week, one of his customers said that he'd pay next week, and another explained that she wanted to pay at the end of every month. Making money wasn't quite as easy as he'd thought.

He offered Billie the thirty dollars he'd collected.

"No way," she said. "You earned it. It's yours."

"I want to pay my way."

"You help me around the house, you cut the grass, that's enough. Save your money for school clothes. As soon as you have enough, I'll take you to the bank, you can put it in there. It takes a hundred dollars."

He couldn't make her change her mind. "Okay," he said at last. "I'll save it, use my baby-sitting money for gas and oil and the movies." And a few bags of marshmallows.

"Don't save it all," Billie said. "I want you to get a haircut. You need one real bad."

He nodded. "I'll get a crew cut."

"It's none of my business," Billie said, "but you keep saying your ears stick out. A crew cut's going to draw attention to that."

"If I have them leave it longer, I have to get it cut again in a few weeks."

"Suit yourself," Billie said. "It just seems to me it's worth it to feel like you look better."

He asked the barber to cut it short at the sides and on the neck, but to leave enough at the front for him to comb back. When the barber finished, Jim surveyed himself critically in the mirror. Maybe it helped a little, but he was still ugly. He realized that he hadn't thought much lately about how he looked; he'd been too busy.

Buddy kept urging him to buy a bike. "We could go bike riding, you had a bike," he said every day, and every day Jim retorted, "We could go to Mars, we had a flying saucer."

Privately, he wished that he could buy a bike. But he knew that they cost over a hundred dollars, even two hundred, and he wanted to save his money. In August, when Billie's girls came back and Troy moved out, he was going to pay several weeks' rent in advance on the spare room, all the money he had except what he needed for a couple of pairs of new jeans for school.

On Sundays he and Buddy rode in the back of Troy's truck to the lake to go swimming. Buddy was a good swimmer. As June slipped into July, and July headed toward August, Jim felt his own strokes become cleaner and stronger as they raced each other out into the lake and back.

One Sunday afternoon, on their way to the lake, Troy detoured past Southside Garage, where he worked, and pointed out a man's bicycle in the window of the office. One of the customers had brought it in. There was a For Sale sign on it. "It's like brand new," Troy said. "He wants seventy-five dollars, but I think he'll take fifty. He needs the money."

The bike of Jim's dreams was a freewheeler, all chrome, that would outshine Buddy's racy yellow model. This bike was a plain black nothing. But it would let him get around and do errands for Billie.

"Okay," he said. "For fifty bucks I'll buy it."

"Yea!" Buddy cried. "Now we can go bike riding!"

"I'll call the guy tomorrow," Troy promised.

He was an ally now, a combination of friend and big brother and father. It made Jim ashamed to remember that once he'd thought he hated him. Now he wished that Troy didn't have to move out, that the three of them could go on living in Billie's house forever. They were like a family, even though Troy went out on dates some nights. That disturbed Jim, as if it were an act of disloyalty.

"I should think he'd want to save his money," he complained to Billie later that afternoon, after they came home from swimming and Troy left for what he called Mexican and a movie with a girl named Darlene.

"Everybody needs some fun in their life."

"You don't go out on dates," he pointed out.

"I don't have the time."

"Would you if you did?"

"I don't know, Jim. Right now I have all I can handle."

In a month her daughters would fly home from Atlanta. Maybe the plane would crash. It was a terrible thought; he didn't want them to die, or Billie to be unhappy.

All he wanted was for things to go on exactly the way they were now.

# CHAPTER 13

The next day Troy brought the bicycle home in the back of his truck. He came into the kitchen while Jim was making a sandwich for lunch, and said that the owner would take fifty dollars for it. Jim practiced riding it before he went to Ben's to read his mail. Two years ago, when he began to grow tall, he'd outgrown the child's bike Grandma had given him one Christmas. She couldn't afford to buy him a bigger one. Jim was afraid that he'd forget how to ride, and Grandma said that was something you never forgot. He found out that afternoon, as he practiced in front of Billie's house, that she was right. If anything, he rode even better now that he had a bike that was the right size.

"That is one fine bike," Ben said admiringly after Jim rode down the street and performed wheelies for him and Trudie.

They went to take their nap. Jim killed time riding up and down the dirt road, then bumped over the lawn and onto the boat dock. The sky was overcast; there had been rain every afternoon since the day of the big thunderstorm. He stood on the end of the dock, holding his bike, scanning the choppy gray waves. A thrill went through him that made his heart jump when he spotted, a few yards out to his right, the familiar double hump of the alligator's bony eyebrows.

"Hey, Gator, see what I have here?" he called across the water. "You want a ride? You'd look kind of funny on a bike with your short little legs!"

The mental vision made him laugh. He laid down his bike and pulled a bag of marshmallows from his pocket. The spectacle of his friend's cruel jaws snapping up the soft white candies filled him with excitement and a feeling of power. If he could control an alligator in the wild, he could control his own life.

He rode no-hands into Buddy's carport. Buddy echoed Jim's wild Indian yell and jumped onto his own bicycle. All afternoon they explored the dirt roads beyond Ben's house. Jim got home just before Billie drove in from work, and ran outside to meet her.

"That's great," she said after he performed on his bike for her. She looked tired. Inside, kicking off her shoes, she said, "I got mad at a client on the phone today. My boss heard me, made me call him back and apologize. Then she said maybe I better make a choice between my day job and my night job, because it looks like I can't handle both."

"She's mean," Jim said. The microwave oven pinged. He took out Billie's coffee and handed it to her.

"She's right," Billie responded. "She wants me to go to school at night so I can be a paralegal, make more money. I told her if ever I get ahead a little bit, I'll just work weekends at the restaurant, start back to Valencia." It was the name of the local community college. "I used to take classes there before I got married."

"I can help out," Jim said. "I'm making fifty dollars a week, and I got eighteen for baby-sitting last week. I can make more if I do more lawns."

"You're doing enough lawns," she said, "and you need your money for yourself. I'll be taking you back to Tampa next month."

Troy came in and looked at their gloomy faces. "What's wrong?" he asked. "Jim get in trouble? Is it because I got him the bike?"

"No it's not," Billie snapped. "I'm just explaining the facts of life to him."

"About sending him back to Tampa? You can't do that, Billie. He told me there's this real creepy guy wants to take him in."

"Over my dead body! He's going to his relatives in Georgia."

"He said nobody knows where they are."

"His aunt's trying to find them. Whatever happens, he's not going to Fred."

"He belongs here," Troy said. "You and him get along real well."

Billie didn't answer as she went to the kitchen to start dinner. But it boosted Jim's spirits to know

81

that he had somebody on his side. Maybe, if he kept quiet and Troy kept speaking up, none of the things he feared would happen. Billie wouldn't send him away, Troy wouldn't have to leave, life would go on forever the way it was now. He wondered if hope was in his genes, passed down from Grandma.

Now that he had a bike, he and Buddy rode every afternoon, up and down the dirt roads, around the new houses under construction, into the old orange grove that was being cut up into lots, where Buddy said there was a million dollars buried. Jim knew the neighborhood now better than Billie did, better, probably, than her lazy kids. It was his neighborhood; he belonged.

It seemed to him that week that Billie was quieter than usual, less ready with smart answers to the problems in her life. Once he asked if she was going to lose her job.

"No," she said. "I had a talk with my boss. I guess I got my priorities straight. I talked to her about some other things too." She stopped abruptly, as if she might say something he shouldn't hear. "I better get dinner," she said, and went to the kitchen with a frown on her face and her lips pressed together.

On Sunday afternoon Buddy came down to go to the lake with them. He and Jim and Troy shot baskets while Billie made her weekly call to her daughters. They heard her hang up the telephone.

"You ready, Billie?" Troy called through the door.

She came to the door, unsmiling. "I need to talk to Jim," she said. "It won't take long."

Jim sat down with her at the table in the dining area. She looked so serious that he felt afraid. Maybe she didn't call her girls. Maybe she talked to Aunt Bessie and there was a relative in Georgia ready to take him. He wouldn't go, he'd run away if she sent him—

"I talked to my girls," Billie said, "about having you stay here."

He held his breath, afraid to believe what he was hearing.

"I couldn't live with myself if I sent you away," she said. "It would be like sending one of my own kids. I'd always be wondering what you were doing, if you were happy. I talked to HRS last week, asked them about adopting you."

Happiness rose in his eyes and spread across his face in an idiotic grin as he looked at her.

"They said first you'd have to be made a ward of the state," Billie continued. "Then they think I could qualify to be your foster mother. That way you'd be covered for medical, and they'd pay me to look after you. Just for a while, then if we're all getting along, I'd apply to adopt you, and you could go on my health insurance." Across the table, she held his eyes in her own brown stare, bringing him down to earth. "How do you feel about it?" she asked.

"I think it's great." His voice sounded thin, as

inadequate as his words. He was smiling, and at the same time had tears in his eyes. "I think it's just great," he said.

"Now don't get excited," Billie warned. "It might not work out, but my girls said they'll try, and I'll sure try, and I know you'll try."

Her words reached him from far away. He was floating on air, hearing her and at the same time ignoring her warning that it might not work out. It was going to work out. Grandma and Aunt Bessie were right. You kept on hoping and things worked out.

"Jim?" Billie said. "You hear me? It's not going to be easy. You never had sisters before, my girls never had a brother. We'll all have to give and take."

"Yes ma'am." He'd give and they could take. He'd do anything he had to do. Those girls could walk all over him.

Troy's voice broke into his happy trance, yelling to them to come on and get to the lake before it was time to come home.

"That's great," he said when Jim rushed out and told him the news. "I'll help out. I'll come and get you when I move to my apartment, take you swimming. Maybe we can go to a Magic game."

That was the only flaw in Jim's happiness, that Troy wouldn't be part of the family unit. For one second he yearned for his old dream, of himself and Billie and Troy living happily ever after, always together. He brushed aside the thought. He was staying, that was all that mattered.

It was the kind of day that nothing could spoil. At the lake, they raced back and forth and played games in the water. Billie and Troy went halves on a bucket of fried chicken on the way home, and Buddy called his mother to ask if he could stay for supper. While he was on the telephone, Jim began to set the table. The sky was darkening for the rain that came now every afternoon; Billie went to put their wet towels in the dryer. Troy was outside, tracking down a noise in the motor of his truck.

"Man oh man!" Buddy yelled into the telephone. "Oh gee, I have to tell Jim! Okay, I will, okay!"

"Can you eat with us?" Jim asked as his friend hung up. Buddy's outburst, probably over some trivial family happening, was typical of his little-boy behavior.

"Yeah, but wait till you hear! A gator came out the lake and ate old man Morrison's dog! Can you believe that? Gee, I wish I was there!"

A terrible coldness rushed into Jim, and a terrible weight crushed his heart. He stood as if he were paralyzed, while the meaning of what Buddy had said crashed over him. The gator, his gator, his friend, had killed Trudie. It had come that afternoon, as it came every afternoon, expecting marshmallows, and when it didn't find them it found the little dog instead. His fault, his fault, his fault.

The plates in his hand slipped onto the carpet. From far away, as if there were balls of cotton in his ears, he heard a roll of thunder. He stared at Buddy, but all he saw was the flash of snapping jaws, the teeth like thick white nails, Trudie trotting along with her tail wagging, seized in that long cruel mouth. . . .

"Let's go up there!" Buddy cried. "Let's go see can we see the gator! Hey, maybe they caught it!"

Jim turned on him in a fury. "You big stupid!" he cried. "Stupid stupid stupid!"

Blindly, he lashed out with clenched fists, and felt their impact on Buddy's big soft body. Buddy yelled and hit back; they were pummeling each other when Troy ran in and pulled them apart.

"What in the world?" he cried, and behind him Billie called out, "What's going on?"

"He hit me," Buddy hollered. "I'm going home!"

He started for the door. Billie and Troy tried to stop him as they asked what was wrong. Jim dashed away from them, down the hall and into his room. He locked the door and flung himself facedown on his bed. Outside, the rain pounded on the roof. He heard thunder, and the crackle that meant that lightning had struck something.

Someone tapped on his door and tried the doorknob. "Jim," Billie called. "Troy took Buddy home. Now, what's this all about?"

He didn't answer, pressing his face into the pillow to stem his tears. She called again, pleading with him to unlock his door. He wished that the pillow would suffocate him, to stop the pain growing so big inside him that he thought he'd explode. He wished she'd stop calling his name. Didn't she know that his throat was blocked by a grief too big to swallow? Didn't she understand that, even if he could speak, he couldn't describe to anybody the awful pictures in his mind?

# CHAPTER 14

Eventually Billie went away. Jim stayed facedown
on his bed. Subconsciously, without seeing the early
evening sun steal back into his room, he was aware
that the rain had stopped. Somewhere in the house
were voices, Troy's and Billie's.

Billie came to his door again, tapped and tried the
knob. Her voice was soft as she called his name.
"Jim. Buddy told Troy about Mr. Morrison's dog. I'm
real sorry. I guess you were real fond of her."

His tears flowed again.

"Open the door, Jim. You been by yourself long
enough. Come on, let me in."

He'd never cried so hard in his life. Blinded, he
rolled over to the edge of the bed, sat up, and felt for
the little button that locked the door. After he
unlocked it, he rolled back onto his side with his
face to the wall. He felt the pressure of Billie's body
as she sat down on his bed. She patted his shoulder.

"She'd drown, Jim," she said. "That little dog'd be
dead before she knew what was happening to her.
She wouldn't suffer."

He could imagine Trudie's terror as the jaws closed around her, the awful feeling of not being able to breathe as she was held under the water. He'd told Ben he'd take care of her. . . . His body writhed, and he shook his head from side to side, facedown on the rosy spread.

"Look at it this way," Billie said. "She was thirteen years old. That's a good life for a dog. She died while she still enjoyed living. She was down on the beach doing what she loved to do."

"It was my fault," Jim said. His voice was between a croak and a whisper. He turned over and sat halfway up, not looking into Billie's face, seeing nothing but a blur of wall and roses. "I fed the gator," he said. "I gave it marshmallows. I had it coming every day, then on the weekends I wasn't there."

There was silence. Billie was in shock, washing her hands of him. Who'd want to adopt a kid that fed a gator?

She put her arms around him. "That was real stupid, Jim," she said. "You know better than that." Strangely, her saying the things he'd been saying to himself, with her arms around him, was more comforting than if she'd tried to deny them. "Okay, a lot of people do stupid things, including me. You do them and you pay for them and you get over them."

"If I didn't feed the gator, it wouldn't have got Trudie!"

"You did wrong feeding it. The rest we don't know about."

He twisted in her embrace so that he was looking into her face. She was still wearing the terry-cloth wrap she'd put on over her swimsuit. "If Ben knew I fed the gator, he wouldn't have let Trudie go down by the water. He'll hate me!"

"Let's go tell him," Billie said. "I'll go with you. I already called somebody to work for me tonight."

"I can't. I don't want to!"

She sat back from him. "It looks to me like you have two choices. You can tell him, and maybe have to live with him not liking you anymore, or you can not tell him, and have to live with that."

"It's the worst thing I ever did in my whole life!"

"You didn't want it to happen. You did something stupid, like me when I refinanced my house, like Troy running up all those bills."

"You didn't hurt anybody else."

"I hurt my kids," Billie said. "I told them how it happened, and they said it was okay, but they'll be the ones hurt if I lose this house."

She had brought a box of tissues with her. Jim reached for them and blew his nose. His face felt as if there was a tight film of plastic over it.

"I'll go tell him," he said.

"I'll go with you."

"No." He was afraid he might change his mind halfway there, and Billie would argue with him in the street. "I have to do it myself."

"Okay," she said. "I'll wait here."

He took a long time to wash his face, and killed

more time combing his hair back and forth, waiting for the redness around his eyes to fade away. There was a certain relief in having made a decision, but there was also a black fear as to how Ben would react to his confession. He'd give anything not to have to live through the next hour, to close his eyes and open them again and have this dreadful day, which had started out so well, behind him.

When he went through the living room, Troy and Billie were sitting on the couch. Troy half rose, and Billie pulled him back. Jim nodded to them.

"I'm going," he said.

By now it was dark. The world matched his mood as he walked down the street, forcing himself to place one foot in front of the other. Ben's house was a pale blur in the dark night. Jim went down the side to the back. The living room light was on, throwing a bright white square over the silent porch.

He went up the steps and across the porch, and tapped on the door. In other times Trudie would have alerted Ben with her furious barking. . . . He tapped again, and heard movement from inside. Choking back his panic, he waited while Ben went through the motions of unlocking the door. It opened. Ben stood there in his khaki pants and white T-shirt. Without his hat, his hair was white and wispy. He stood on the other side of the screen door and didn't invite Jim in, remembering, apparently, that Jim's aunt didn't allow him in other people's houses.

"Well," he said, "it's you, boy." The little room

behind him was full of furniture bought a long time ago. His voice trembled. There was on his face an expression of such deep sorrow that Jim thought instinctively of his own feelings the night Grandma died. "I guess you heard what happened," Ben said. "What happened to my Trudie."

"Yes sir." He was panting, as if he'd run all the way.

"Wa'n't a thing I could do," Ben said. "It were all over 'fore I knew what was happening. I never let her near the water, but there was a beer can down there some slob tossed out his boat, washed up on my beach. I went down to get it. Trudie was behind me, sniffing around like she does. All of a sudden I heard her yell. When I looked around, it had her in its mouth, dragging her under. That's the last I seen her."

"I'm sorry," Jim wept. "I'm real sorry."

"I know you are," Ben said. "I know you loved Trudie. Miz Gruber down the street called the sheriff, they told the Game and Fish Commission. They're sending a trapper tomorrow, try to catch that gator. It won't bring Trudie back."

Jim stood in front of him, shaking his head from side to side.

"I appreciate you coming," Ben said.

He was ready to close the door. Jim forced the words out of his throat in one gigantic leap.

"It was my fault, I fed the gator, I gave it marshmallows every afternoon and then on Sundays I didn't come, I'm sorry, I'm real sorry!"

Ben was silent, as if he didn't believe what he was hearing. "You fed that gator?" he said at last.

"Yes sir. I went down on your dock every day while you and Trudie took your nap. I'm sorry." He said it over and over, "I'm sorry, I'm real sorry." Behind the screen, behind his glasses, Ben struggled with his emotions.

"You didn't ought to done that, boy," he said at last.

"I know. It's my fault Trudie died."

"I know you wouldn't hurt her on purpose, but I told you how gators love dogs, and I showed you that gator out there. I told you how some durn fools feed 'em marshmallows." He stopped abruptly. "Is that where you got the idea?" he asked.

"Yes sir, but if you didn't tell me, I'd prob'ly have fed it anyway, bread or some such thing."

"Why did you do it?"

"I felt sorry for it. It's ugly."

"They're not people."

"No sir."

"What time did you feed it?"

"Right after you and Trudie lay down for your nap."

"One-thirty, two o'clock. I'll tell the trapper to be here then. Maybe it'll come looking for you, he can get it."

"Sir?" Jim felt his courage rise and fall, and rise again. "Sir, it wasn't the gator's fault, it was mine. I stop feeding it, it'll stop coming."

"Too late," Ben said. "It's a nuisance gator now. It's lost its fear of man."

"It only came because I fed it. I won't do that anymore. I'll never go down on your dock again, I swear it!"

"Don't waste your pity on a gator," Ben said. "Nasty, ugly things, eat their own young."

"They help keep other animals alive when there's a drought," Jim said in a low voice. Their water holes represented reservoirs at such times. There was no point in trying to explain that to Ben; he wasn't listening.

"Don't you want to get the one that killed Trudie?" he demanded with such anguish in his face that Jim nodded in spite of himself. "I should think so," Ben said. "You could maybe help. You could come here tomorrow around one-thirty, show the trapper where you fed it, give him some idea where to look for it. Will you do that, boy? Will you do that for Trudie?"

"Yes, sir." What else could he say?

"You do that, and I'll know you're sorry."

"Yes, sir." He turned to leave.

"Don't be too hard on yourself, boy," Ben called after him. "I know you wouldn't hurt Trudie on purpose."

Jim trudged home, more miserable than he'd ever been in his life. In redeeming himself, he'd agreed to sacrifice his friend.

# CHAPTER 15

**T**he next morning he kept as busy as he could so that he wouldn't think about what he had to do at 1:30. It didn't work. He thought of nothing else. He made Billie's coffee, yelled outside Buddy's window to make his late-sleeping business partner get up, mowed a lawn on Orange Blossom Lane and another on the next street, took a shower, and ate his lunch, all the time aware that the hour was coming closer for him to betray his friend.

He thought of running away. But he'd be running from the family he'd always wanted. Perhaps that made him realize that the world wouldn't end at 1:30. Today would be hard to get through, but, as Billie told him before she left for work, that was life. You hurt, and then you went on.

At 1:15 her car pulled into the drive.

"Long lunch hour," she said. "I thought you could use a little moral support."

While she was changing her clothes, Troy arrived.

"I figured if I asked, you'd say no," he said, "so I didn't ask."

Jim wanted to go by himself, get it over and done with and never speak of it again. But he found, as he walked down the street in the hot afternoon sun with Billie and Troy on either side of him, that it felt good to have them there. When they drew abreast of the Wellins' house, Buddy came out from the carport. That morning, as they mowed their lawns, he and Jim had hardly spoken to each other. Now he said nothing but "Hi, Miz Newhouse, hi, Troy," and loped along beside Billie.

A small crowd, mostly children and older people, had gathered in Ben's backyard. A murmur ran among them as they parted to make way for Jim and his friends. A pickup truck was parked at the edge of the lake. Ben was walking toward it. It was the first time Jim had seen him down here without Trudie at his heels. Even in the midst of all these people, he looked lonely.

Ben stopped behind the pickup truck to speak to a sturdy, suntanned man in jeans and a peaked cap. The lake was placid. Close to the shore, three men sat in a small motorboat. One of them held a rifle.

Jim swept his eyes back and forth across the lake. No telltale humps broke the glassy surface. Relief surged through him. Maybe the alligator's instincts told it that it had committed a terrible crime, and it would stay away from here forever.

Now he was abreast of Ben and the man in the peaked cap. Introductions were made, of Ben to Billie and Troy, of the other man to all of them. His name was Otis Lampp; he was the trapper sent by the Game and Fresh Water Fish Commission to rid the lake of the nuisance alligator.

"You the one that was feeding it?" he asked Jim.

"Yes sir." It didn't sound like his voice.

"You know that's against the law? You were an adult, you could get sixty days in jail and a five-hundred-dollar fine. How'd you like that?"

"I wouldn't like it, sir. I'm real sorry." He stiffened his spine and pointed to the men in the boat. "Are they going to shoot it?"

"They better not," the trapper said grimly. "Only one time the year they let folks do that, and then only a certain number. State licenses them, lets them kill their limit, sell them for their meat and hides." He projected his voice toward the boat. "You guys hold your fire, you hear? You don't, you'll be in big trouble."

One of the men yelled back, "We're just here to give you some backup, case it gets away."

"It won't get away," the trapper promised. "You just stay out of it."

He turned back toward his truck and took from the back of it a coil of rope looped to form a lasso, a roll of wide white tape, a fishing rod, and a raw chicken the size that Grandma used to cut up and fry. He laid everything out on the edge of the dock and stood in the shallow water next to it.

"Everybody up on the dock," he ordered.

Jim and his friends climbed up there. Ben went to

the end and walked back, through the people clustered above the trapper.

"What are you going to do?" Jim asked. He stood on the dock, watching the trapper's every movement.

"First off, I want you to show me where it comes. Where was it when you fed it?"

Jim had always thrown the marshmallows to the right of the dock, a few yards out. He pointed to the left.

"How far out?" the trapper asked.

"Real far," Jim lied.

"Wa'n't far the day I seen it," Ben said. "Wa'n't more'n a few yards, out there." He pointed into the lake, on the right side of the dock.

"How about that, boy?" the trapper asked. "That where you fed it?"

Jim nodded, a slight movement that felt like the kiss of Judas. "Are you going to kill it?" he asked.

"Depends how big it is. Under six feet, I'll take it to some lake out in the boondocks, no houses around."

"What if it's bigger'n that? Are you going to kill it?"

"You have to strike a balance," the trapper said. "For a long time gators were protected because folks were killing them so fast it looked like they'd become extinct. Now there's so many of them they sometimes get to be a nuisance, like this one. Most of the time, you leave them alone they'll leave you alone, but this is the nesting season, when they lay their eggs. That's when they get rambunctious."

"I wish I never seen it out there," Jim said in a low voice.

"It won't be out there much longer," Otis Lampp said. "That's where it comes, huh?" He gestured on the right side of the dock.

Jim stood mute.

"You like that gator, boy?" Ben challenged him.

It's my friend. The words stuck in his throat.

"How did you feel when Trudie died?" Ben snapped.

"Real bad, sir."

"You feel that way 'bout that gator?"

"Yes sir."

"Trudie were better'n any gator," the old man said. "I never thought I could miss anybody like I miss her. Don't waste your pity on a gator, boy."

"No sir."

He wanted to leave, but a sense of loyalty kept him standing there on the dock, with Billie and Troy and Buddy and Ben close beside him. He was responsible for turning the alligator into a killer. Now he had to stay here, to suffer with it.

The crowd of people straggling along the dock moved closer. Jim heard the excitement in their voices as the trapper threw the chicken, on the end of his fishing line, a few yards out into the lake. Then, with the rope looped over one wrist, he cupped his hand over his mouth and made a series of grunts as he stood there in the shallow water. That must be how a gator sounded, Jim realized. He felt hypnotized as he gazed into the lake, toward the spot where, every afternoon, he'd seen the humps. Stay away, he prayed.

His spirits rose as the lake surface remained calm. The trapper continued to grunt his treacherous love call. Suddenly, a few yards out, there was a movement, and the alligator's bony eyebrows rose above the smooth gray water. The trapper grunted again and pulled gently on his fishing line. The humps submerged. Let it go home, Jim prayed, don't let it smell the chicken.

But the love call and the movement of the bait were powerful lures. The fishing line snapped taut as the submerged alligator swallowed its prey in one gulp. The trapper jerked on his rod and began to reel in. The alligator thrashed in the water, to the accompaniment of a cheer from the watching crowd. Men jumped down from the dock and waded into the water. The trapper waved them back.

"I can handle it," he said, and reeled in the struggling reptile as it pitched and plunged at the end of his line. He hauled it into water a couple of inches deep. It was hard for Jim to judge the length of the scaly body as the tail lashed back and forth. The thrashing animal wasn't the enormous beast Swift Panther had ridden to the bottom of the lake, but how long was six feet? A man lying down—the comparison was useless, he realized, as he watched his friend's defeat.

Swiftly, Otis Lampp threw his rope in a noose over the long broad mouth and pulled it tight. He seized the bound jaws and flipped the alligator onto its back. It stopped struggling. The trapper dragged it out of the water and onto the grass. Willing hands held out his tape; he strapped it around the animal's jaws, around its throat, behind its eyes. It lay there quietly. People jumped down from the dock and crowded around it. A child stretched out her hand toward the soft white belly and quickly withdrew it.

"Long as it's on its back, it can't move," a man said, and now a dozen hands reached out.

"Stay back," the trapper ordered, and everyone moved back an inch or two.

Jim jumped down onto the grass, beside the helpless alligator. Its belly had the look of a mosaic made with small white tiles. The rest of its skin was grayish black, and scaly. The upper teeth protruded over the lower jaw, long and sharp and far apart.

"How long is it?" he asked the trapper.

"Around six foot, I guess. I'll take it out Lake Nellie. Nothing out there 'cept water moccasins and gators."

"Can he go with you?" Billie asked. She'd jumped down from the dock after Jim, followed by Troy and Buddy.

The trapper hesitated, then shrugged. "Guess it won't do no harm," he said. "You want to do that, Jim?"

"Yes sir!" Relief rushed through his body like a breath of air. Going with the alligator to its new home wouldn't excuse him for what he'd done to it, for causing its separation from mate and family and from the lake where it had lived its life. But at least he wouldn't have to wonder forever and ever if it was killed or set free. And Ben had said that if he came here today to help the trapper, he'd be forgiven his part in Trudie's death. That would go a long way toward helping him forgive himself.

The afternoon seemed brighter, although dark clouds were gathering above the trees. Jim raised his eyes to look at Billie and Troy and Buddy.

"I'm real glad you came," he said.

"No sweat," Troy replied, and Billie squeezed his hand. Buddy said, "I'm sorry I made you mad yesterday."

"That's okay. I'm sorry I got mad."

Otis Lampp seized the gator's tail and, with one gigantic heave, flipped it into the back of his pickup. He got in and started the motor. Jim got in on the other side and rode off with him.

# CHAPTER 16

His ordeal wasn't quite over. That evening before Billie left for work a deputy sheriff came to lecture him and to warn him that if he broke the law again, he'd end up in juvenile court. He was lucky, she said, that both Mr. Morrison and Otis Lampp thought he'd learned his lesson.

"Yes, ma'am," Jim said fervently, and breathed a sigh of relief when she left.

A normal routine meant going to Ben's house the following afternoon. During the morning, while he mowed lawns, he thought of a thousand reasons not to go. But after he brought in Billie's mail he started up the street on his bike. He might as well know now how Ben felt about him.

The sight of Ben beside his mailbox, without Trudie, was devastating. He looked smaller and older. Maybe his shoulders had always sagged; today they seemed to droop almost to his waist. Jim crossed the road and stood in front of him.

"Hi, Mr. Morrison."

"Afternoon," Ben said. He stood there for a moment, leafing through his mail. "Junk," Jim heard him mutter. "Garbage. Straight into the trash can." He held out one long typewritten envelope. "What's this, boy?" he asked.

Ben didn't hate him! The tension inside him dissolved as he took the envelope and read aloud the return address. "Benefit Insurance Company, forty-two oh two Main Street . . ."

"Garbage," Ben said, and took the letter back. "Thank you, boy," he said, and started toward his house.

Without Trudie. That thought led to another. "Sir," Jim called. He laid down his bicycle and hurried up to Ben as the old man paused and turned. "Would you want another dog?" he asked.

"You know somebody has one?"

"No, sir, but I could find out."

"My daughter said she'd get me one," Ben said. "She's coming in September."

"I can get you one before then!" Jim cried.

He bicycled home with ideas spinning in his head, bypassing Buddy's house for the moment, diverted from his sadness that there was no alligator to visit that afternoon. He had money in the bank, he'd buy Ben the best dog there was, the most expensive, a big dog, a beautiful dog that could win prizes, Irish setter, German shepherd, buy him a real good collar, real leather, with brass studs if Ben wanted them, with diamonds if they made them that way!

"That's a real good thing to do," Billie said when he spilled out his plan after she came home from work. She kicked off her shoes and sipped her coffee. "You know, they have dogs at the county shelter. They have to put them to sleep if nobody wants them. They give them their shots, spay them, everything, you pay for it."

"What kind of dogs?" Jim asked. Not the kind that would cost enough to make him stop feeling guilty, he thought.

"All kinds. Why don't you ask Mr. Morrison what kind he wants?"

Ben didn't even stop to consider when Jim put the question to him the next afternoon.

"Little dog like Trudie," he said. "I got her from the shelter."

"You wouldn't want a Labrador?" Jim asked. "There's a lady in the paper has some puppies."

"Eat me out of house and home," Ben said. "I like a dog can jump up in my lap."

Jim shrugged off his disappointment. "My aunt says we can go Saturday morning," he said. "You want to come, pick it out yourself?"

And so on Saturday morning Billie drove Jim and Ben to the animal shelter to buy a dog like Trudie. A female, Ben said, because they were easier to train. There were what looked like hundreds of dogs, males and females, all sizes and colors, barking in wire-walled pens. The one Ben chose was a nondescript white dog with black patches on her back and around one eye, a scrawny animal, nothing like the dog of Jim's dreams.

"This one," Ben said. "She's so homely, we don't take her nobody will."

It seemed a good reason to choose a dog. "What are you going to call her?" Jim asked.

"Patches," Ben said. "That's her name, Patches."

He made an appointment for her to be spayed and inoculated the week that his daughter was coming. Jim paid for it; it was only $23.50, because Ben got a 50 percent senior citizen discount.

On the way home Ben held Patches in his lap in the front seat, beside Billie, with the window open so that the dog could stick her nose out. They stopped at McDonald's and all of them, including Patches, had a hamburger.

The burgers and french fries and milk shakes and coffee came to $8.34. Jim paid the bill. He wanted to spend more, but you couldn't estimate Ben's joy in dollars and cents. He'd always remember Trudie, but he was over his grief. Remembering the pain and the guilt and the trouble he'd caused, Jim wasn't quite over his.

The moment he came into view on his bicycle that afternoon, Patches raced across the dirt road to greet him. Younger and livelier than Trudie, she was also less obedient; Trudie had never crossed the road unless Ben went with her.

"Bad girl, Patches!" Ben cried as he hurried after her with a leash in his hands. He'd never have caught her except that she stopped when she reached Jim and leaped into the air with all four feet off the ground as she scrabbled at his jeans.

"Bad girl, Patches," Jim echoed. He dropped his bike and held her so that Ben could hook the leash onto the collar that used to be Trudie's.

"I'm going to have to keep you on this till you learn your manners," Ben scolded. He patted her before he stood up. Released from his hold, Patches dashed back across the road, tugging him after her.

"She giving you trouble?" Jim asked. He was disappointed; he wanted the dog he gave Ben to be perfect.

"Nobody ever bothered with her," Ben said. "How would you be if your grandma didn't tell you right from wrong?"

"Did you have to train Trudie?"

"Sure did, or maybe she trained me." He laughed, and took his mail out of the box while Patches ran in circles and tangled the leather strap that held her back. "Don't you worry about Patches," he said. "Her and me'll get along just fine."

"I'm still sorry about Trudie," Jim said. "I wish it never happened."

"I know you do, boy. But if it didn't, Patches would have been put to sleep, so something good come out of it."

Jim thought about it on the way to Buddy's. It seemed a harsh exchange, one dog living because another died. But then, the change in his own life happened because his grandma died. The difference was that there was nothing he could have done to prevent Grandma's death, but he felt responsible for Trudie's.

His gator could have been killed too. Through pure luck, it survived to live out its life in its natural habitat. Lake Nellie was an isolated place, surrounded by palmetto scrub and a few lonely palm trees. The only sign of civilization was the rutted track fishermen had made as they drove their vehicles from the county road. When the trapper released the alligator on the edge of the lake, it headed into the water without a moment's pause. The ripples it made lasted less than a second as it disappeared into the weeds under the surface. It was back where it belonged, in the Florida that existed before people surrounded lakes with houses.

That didn't excuse him for feeding it. But it taught him that, sometimes, things worked out for the best. He'd been lucky. It was a good feeling, one that gave him hope that other things would work out too.

At the same time, he felt a sense of loss, the way he'd felt when Grandma died. A part of his life was gone. He'd miss his afternoon visits to the lake. One day, when he was grown and had a car, he was going to drive out to Lake Nellie and stand beside the water and tell his gator how sorry he was that he'd fed it.

Maybe he'd see it. Maybe it would still surface, day after day, showing itself in those silent humps above the water, waiting for marshmallows to float out to it. Maybe it didn't know that it was in a different lake, with different alligators. But if it had a mate, it would miss it, wouldn't it?

When he was back in school, he'd get books on alligators from the library and find out all he could about them. Until then he'd fill up his afternoons with something else. As Billie said, you made mistakes and you paid for them, and then you got on with your life.

Before he got on with his, there was another change to deal with. Troy had found a studio apartment he could afford and was moving out. In his heart Jim wished for the good old days, when he and Billie and Troy lived in her house, and Trudie lived with Ben, and the alligator lived in Ben's lake. But back then, he was supposed to go back to Tampa at the end of the summer.

On the day Troy moved, Jim went with him to see his apartment. It was small and plainly furnished, with a couch that made into a bed. There was a swimming pool behind the two-story building. After they moved in Troy's belongings, they went swimming.

"I'll pick you up after work some days, take you out to supper, then we'll go swimming," Troy promised on the way back to Billie's house.

"I wish you didn't have to move out," Jim said.

Troy laughed. "Little while back you wished I didn't move in," he pointed out.

"I know. But I wish when things get to be the way you want them, they stayed that way."

That night, while Billie was at work, Jim moved his clothes into Troy's room, his room now. Then he vacuumed the room he'd vacated, straightened the books on the bookshelves, and polished the furniture, so that his cousins wouldn't have one thing to complain about. In the morning, when he gave Billie her coffee, he said again, "I wish Troy didn't have to move out."

"You wish we were a family, don't you?" Billie asked. She slowed her rush to the door. "Just you and me and Troy, without my girls coming home."

How did she know about his fantasy? He felt ashamed for wanting it.

"Troy has his own life to live," Billie said. "He's a nice guy, but that don't mean I need to marry him. We'll do okay. My girls are pretty nice kids."

"They won't like me. They're cute."

"I thought you got over that. I thought you told me you're glad Mr. Morrison picked that homely little dog."

"It's different with dogs. They don't even know how they look."

"You look a whole lot better since you got that haircut, and you're a good kid. That's all that matters, right? Right?" she persisted when he didn't answer.

"Yes ma'am."

"You don't sound like you're convinced. Look, if

you have to leave here it'll be because we're not getting along, not because of the way anybody looks."

He was going to do everything he could to get along, but what about her daughters? Right this minute, up in Atlanta, they were getting ready to come home and meet this kid their mother raved about. He remembered how he felt when Grandma and Aunt Bessie told him about kids that were perfect.

He didn't want to have anything to do with them.

# CHAPTER 17

**T**he fact that it was his first visit to an airport should have made Wednesday evening exciting, except that he was preoccupied with his fears that Billie's daughters would hate him on sight. He and Billie rode the elevated tram high above the ground, from the main building to the terminal where the plane from Atlanta would land. Below them the palm trees and ponds looked like the landscaping that came with toy train sets. Beyond, wide bands of cement stretched out to the horizon and made the world look flat.

It wasn't enough to distract him from the ordeal ahead. He repeated the girls' names in his mind, to get used to saying them. Jennifer. Lorraine. Hi, Jennifer. Hi, Lorraine. He wouldn't hug them unless they hugged him first. Maybe he ought to, maybe they'd wait for him to do it and think he was stuck-up if he didn't. He was going to get along with them even if it killed him. But what if Billie didn't feel the same about him when she got her daughters back? What was he going to do about that?

They arrived early at gate 44, which was really a door in a wall behind rows of chairs. Billie squeezed his arm when the arrival of the flight from Atlanta was announced, and pulled him with her to stand with a small crowd of people in front of the gate as the passengers began to straggle through it. Suddenly she yelled and sprinted forward, and the two girls in the photographs ran out and hugged her.

The younger one, Lorraine, blond and chunky in wide green shorts and a blue T-shirt, jumped up and down. Jennifer, the pretty one, as tall as he was, in jeans and a red top, had tears in her eyes as she embraced her mother. Billie drew Jim into their circle with her arm around his shoulders.

"This is Jim," she said. "I told you about him."

"Hi," Jim said. He started to hold out his hand, and withdrew it as Lorraine launched herself at him with open arms. Her hug reminded him of a teddy bear he had when he was little; she raised her head, which was under his chin, as if to kiss him. Confused, he let his arms drop to his side and gazed over her head at her sister.

"Hi," Jennifer said, and gave him a brief hug as Lorraine, giggling and chattering, moved away.

He heaved a sigh of relief. He'd got through meeting them, not too coolly, but at least it was over. He trudged behind them as they started toward the tram, with Jennifer walking beside her mother and Lorraine dancing around and waving her hand in the air. There was a ring with a clear bluish green stone on one of her pudgy fingers.

"Daddy gave us rings with our birthstones," Jennifer said. "Mine's a real ruby."

She held out her hand. A tiny red chip glinted in the gold ring around one finger.

"It's real pretty," Billie said.

"But you wish he bought us our school clothes instead," Jennifer interjected. "We can buy them ourselves with the money we made baby-sitting our dear little baby brother." Even from behind, Jim caught the sarcasm in her tone and the movement of her cheek as she made a face.

"He's so cute," Lorraine cried.

"He's spoiled rotten," Jennifer said. "The minute he cries, you have to pick him up. Now we're not there, the child bride is getting a full-time baby-sitter."

"Daddy told you not to call her that," Lorraine observed. "'Her name is Tammy, and that's what you'll call her.'" Her imitation of a man's deep voice was so comical that Jim felt a smile cross his face, in spite of his mixed-up feelings.

They reached the tram platform and waited with a group of passengers from the girls' flight. When the tram came, Lorraine entered by a different door from the rest of them and rode to the terminal in a different compartment.

"She's been that way the whole summer," Jennifer said. "What a brat."

"It's great having you home again," Billie said. "I really missed you. I was lucky I had Jim."

"Did he sleep in our room?"

"I didn't touch your stuff," he said. "Except I read some of your books."

"Where's he going to sleep now?" Jennifer asked. "I thought you had a roomer."

"He moved out," Billie said. "Jim's in there now."

"Daddy thinks you're out of your mind to take on another child," Jennifer observed, and Billie retorted, "It's none of your daddy's business."

The tram stopped, and Lorraine danced up to them. They went to the luggage pickup to get the girls' bags. On the way home, Jennifer sat in front with her mother and Lorraine in the backseat with Jim.

Jennifer twisted in her seat to ask him a question. "What are you going to call Mom?"

"I told him he can call me Mom if he wants to, or whatever he's comfortable with," Billie answered for him. "He don't have to make up his mind right away."

"*Doesn't* have to make up his mind right away," Jennifer said.

She was really something, Jim thought, speaking to her mother as if they were equals, correcting her grammar. Grandma and Aunt Bessie would have said that she was fourteen going on thirty-five. They'd also have told her to stop sassing them, whereas Billie was laughing as she said, "I guess I'll have to be careful now you're back," as if it were okay.

Living in a family was going to be harder than he'd thought. He felt out of place and wondered if his gator felt the same way, getting used to new gators in its life.

He and Billie had agreed in advance to tell the story of Trudie and the alligator before the girls heard it from their friends. Billie let him tell it his own way, sitting around the table with Cokes and cookies after they got home.

"You must be out of your mind!" Jennifer cried when he finished. "Even Lorraine knows better than to feed an alligator!"

"Who says I do?" Lorraine argued. She looked at Jim. "How could it taste a teeny little marshmallow?" she asked, and then, before he could answer, "How do they know they're supposed to like marshmallows?"

"I don't know," Jim said.

"Did you go in the water with it?"

"I stood on Ben's dock."

"Ben? You mean Old Man Morrison?" Jennifer cried. "You went on his property?"

"He's scary," Lorraine said.

"No he's not. I read him his mail every day. I bought him another dog when this happened."

"You think that makes it all right?" Jennifer said sarcastically. "What made you do it in the first place?"

"I was sorry for it. It's ugly."

"So you gave it something," she said. "Did that make you feel better?"

Billie saved him from having to answer. "That's enough about the alligator," she said. "It's a lot better off where it is now, and Jim knows he did wrong, period."

Jim excused himself soon afterward and went to bed. Jennifer's question had upset him. Sure he felt better when he fed the alligator; it made him feel close to it, and in control of something. Talking to it about his problems helped to solve them. But that wasn't why he fed it! He did it to make the gator feel better.

In his mind he saw Jennifer's eyes, as brown and steady as Billie's, when she asked him, "Did it make you feel better?" She knew what she was doing, knew that it would make him ask himself uncomfortable questions. Miss Know-It-All, Grandma and Aunt Bessie would have called her. Miss Buttinski. He was going to keep out of her way.

Later he heard the girls getting ready for bed in the bathroom that used to be his and Troy's. Billie went in to kiss them good night. Through the thin wall he heard Jennifer say that she wished she had her own room.

If he weren't there, she could have. Did she blame

him for that? He fell asleep thinking that it was going to be okay with Lorraine; she was a bit silly, always giggling, but she wouldn't give him any trouble.

Jennifer was going to be the problem in this family.

# CHAPTER 18

The next morning Jim gave Billie her coffee as usual, as she ran through the house dressed for work. He was ready to leave for his first lawn-mowing job when Jennifer came out in shorts and a T-shirt, with Lorraine behind her wearing a short nightgown over bloomers.

"Lorraine, go back and make your bed," Jennifer ordered. She looked at Jim as he stood at the back door. "Did you make yours?"

"I make it every day when I get up, Billie's too. My grandma always made me do that."

Lorraine lay on her back on the couch in the TV room, trying to loop a rubber band over her foot.

"Go make your bed and get dressed," Jennifer said.

"You're not the boss of me!"

"I am when Mom's not here." Jennifer opened one of the kitchen cupboards. "Do you want some cereal?" she asked Jim.

"I already ate. I'm going to mow Miz Spangler's lawn."

"What did you do with your dishes?" Jennifer asked. "We don't use the dishwasher."

"I washed them and put them away."

Lorraine came into the kitchen with the rubber band around her ankle. "Did your grandma make you do that?" she asked.

"She had arthritis," Jim said. "I did all the housework."

"Where is she?"

"She died."

"I'm sorry," Jennifer said. "Mom said you don't have any relatives except us."

"There's one guy, real creepy. If I have to go back, live with him, I'm going to run away and bum on the beach."

"Neat!" Lorraine cried. She stood at the counter, eating cereal from the box.

"You don't have to go back," Jennifer said. "Just remember when Mom's not here, I'm in charge."

She was welcome to be in charge, Jim thought as he trundled his lawn mower toward Buddy's house. He had enough to do with his lawns and his baby-sitting, biking with Buddy, and visiting Ben and Patches. He still missed his afternoon visits to his gator. If he could just have it back he'd never feed it again, just sit on the dock and talk to it.

When he went home for lunch the girls were gone. Jennifer had left him a note, with a telephone number where she could be reached. As if he'd need to call her for permission to do something, he thought.

But he felt better about her, since she'd said that she was sorry his grandma died. She'd also said that he didn't have to leave here, as long as he remembered that she was in charge. She was nice one minute and a pain in the rear the next.

"How you getting along with them gals?" Ben asked that afternoon, and Jim replied, "I guess Lorraine's okay."

The girls were gone all the time, the first few days, as they got in touch with their friends. Lorraine had one whose mother was at home all day. The brother of one of Jennifer's drove them to the mall and the movies, or she had baby-sitting jobs, after she let the neighbors know that she was back. She and Jim had to arrange their baby-sitting, Billie said, so that one of them was at home with Lorraine every night.

In the evenings, if the three of them were together, they argued over which television show to watch. Jennifer made a chart showing whose turn it was to choose. She made another for cleaning the bathroom, and one assigning turns for dishwashing, setting the table, and starting dinner. When Jim said that he didn't know how to cook, she volunteered to teach him. She loved charts, and bossing people around.

Lorraine avoided doing some of her jobs by trading, then forgetting to pay back. Jim let her get away with it. She was so funny. His tolerance upset Jennifer.

"You're not helping her a bit," she said at the end

of the week. "You're letting her think she can go through life being cute and everybody will put up with her."

Lighten up, Jim thought, but didn't say it. He was learning a lot about girls, about families. One of these days he'd be ready to challenge Jennifer, maybe to refuse Lorraine, but not yet.

"You're thinking I'm a real pain in the butt," Jennifer said. "Why don't you say it, instead of being such a goody-goody?"

"I'm just trying to be nice," Jim said angrily.

"Because you think we'll send you away if you speak your mind. You're insecure. I am too, that's why I try to control everything."

"So lighten up."

"I do get uptight," Jennifer conceded. "It's because I'm jealous of the child bride, but I'm working on it."

"You sure know a lot about what's wrong with you."

"They sent me to a psychologist when they got the divorce. Now I can analyze just about anybody. I might go into that field."

"Billie said you were going into computers."

"One or the other."

"Maybe you can analyze computers."

She laughed, not her usual sarcastic laugh but the kind of laugh that showed she had a sense of humor. She wasn't so bad, Jim thought, if you stood up to her.

Troy took him swimming at his apartment some

nights, but not as often as Jim expected. After he brought Jim home one night, Lorraine said that he was cute. She looked at Jim. "You're cute too," she said generously. "I like the way your ears stick out. How'd you get them to do that?"

"Haven't you ever heard of genes?" Jennifer scoffed.

"Sure, I'm wearing them."

"That's what determines how you look, G-E-N-E-S. You get certain ones from each parent. That's why I look like Mom, and you're like Daddy's side of the family. It's nothing you can control. But you can control things like giggling all the time."

Ignoring the slur, Lorraine asked Jim, "Who do you look like?"

Grandma had said that his mother was pretty. "I guess my dad," he said.

He hadn't thought much about it recently. His dad couldn't have looked this bad or his mama wouldn't have married him. He did look better now that he was getting regular haircuts, and he was going to buy contact lenses when he could afford them. But he was never going to be the kind of guy girls went crazy over.

That was okay. His happiness no longer depended on having the whole world approve of him at first glance. People liked people who were good-looking. He couldn't change that, and he wished that he was, but people he didn't know weren't that important anymore. Billie didn't care how he looked, nor Ben nor Troy, not even Jennifer and Lorraine, certainly not Patches, or Trudie, or his gator.

Grandma and Aunt Bessie hadn't cared either. He never thought about it when he lived with them. In his mind, they were old and old-fashioned. He kept quiet and did as he was told and secretly wished that he lived in a regular family.

Now he almost had that family. Billie was going to take formal foster-parent training. Eventually she'd apply to adopt him. It wouldn't be the perfect family he'd dreamed of, where nobody ever got mad. He and Jennifer and Lorraine argued, and sometimes yelled at one another. Billie yelled too, at all of them, when she was tired. But they got over it and said that they were sorry. The worst thing about fighting in this family was that afterward, Jennifer remembered everything you said and told you why you said it, but he was learning to live with that.

HRS—the Department of Health and Rehabilitative Services—needed his birth certificate. Aunt Bessie promised to send it right away when Billie called to tell her the good news that Jim was staying. He grew impatient as he checked the mail every day. To Grandma and Aunt Bessie, right away meant that day or the next time they thought of it, which might be a month later.

There was another reason he needed his birth certificate; Billie had to have it in order to register him for Lakewood High. One part of him looked forward to going back to school after the long vacation.

Another part dreaded the ordeal of transferring to a new one. The only people he'd know there would be Buddy and Jennifer. The other kids, seeing him for the first time, would call him ugly. Accepting the way he looked didn't mean that he was going to enjoy being teased about it.

Buddy had told him that he was called Fatso at school. Since the incident of the alligator, when Buddy stood by him, their friendship was stronger. They still bickered and teased, but they could be serious when one of them had a problem.

"What do you do when the kids call you names?" Jim asked one afternoon when they were biking back from the orange grove.

"Call 'em names back," Buddy replied.

It wasn't the answer Jim was looking for. He got home a few minutes before Billie was due and found Jennifer opening a jar of spaghetti sauce, in accordance with the chart that assigned their evening duties. Lorraine had disappeared, as she usually did when it was her turn to set the table. Jim was down for dishwashing. He'd have set the table too, but he'd made an agreement with Jennifer that Lorraine had to do her part.

He still approached his older cousin as if she were an adult he wasn't quite sure of. She had a way of dragging out of him things he wasn't ready to say, and offering advice he hadn't asked for. But she could be generous; her father was getting her a computer for Christmas, and she said that he could use it. Best of all, she seemed to have an answer for every situation. He told her of his fear that the kids at school would call him ugly.

"Tell them you'll take your smart genes over their good-looking ones any day," she said.

"'N't that conceited?" Jim asked.

"You're trying to shut them up, not start a philosophical discussion," she pointed out. "And wouldn't you rather be smart than good-looking, if you had to make a choice?"

"I'd rather be both," he said. "You are."

"I'm too tall. It'll be all right when I'm an adult, but right now it's a pain."

It was the last week in August. School started the day after Labor Day. "I still don't have my birth certificate," Jim complained.

"You know Mom," Jennifer replied. "If it doesn't come, she'll drive to Tampa to get it."

Her mention of Billie made both of them look at the clock. It was quarter to six. Billie was home every day around five-thirty.

"Maybe she went shopping," Jim suggested, knowing before Jennifer pointed it out that Billie always called if she was going to be late.

Lorraine appeared from wherever she'd been hiding and asked, "Where's Mom?"

"Maybe there's been an accident on I-4," Jennifer said. "That holds up the traffic for hours, at rush hour."

She turned off the microwave oven, where the

126

spaghetti sauce was heating. Jim switched on the television set to one of the stations that included local highway conditions in its early newscast. Five minutes later the telephone rang. Billie said that her car had broken down on I-4, and she'd called Troy to come and get her.

It was over an hour later that he brought her home in the cab of his truck. He'd towed her car to Southside Garage and said that he'd work on it the next evening after work. Billie arranged for someone to take her place at the restaurant that night and the next, and for a ride to her office in the morning.

"I'll fix it so it will go," Troy said, "but it's not worth spending a lot of money on. You need another car, Billie."

This time Billie didn't joke about buying a Mercedes. There was a look of defeat on her face that Jim had never seen there before.

"I can't get to work without a car," she said after Troy left. "As soon as I pay off the roof, I'm going to have to buy one, if I can raise the down payment."

"I have over two hundred dollars in the bank you can have," Jim volunteered.

"I could take some of my school clothes back," Jennifer said, and Lorraine cried, "Me too!"

"You're real sweet," Billie said, "but I have to find a whole new way of life." They were at the table. The spaghetti sauce had been cooked too long, and the spaghetti not long enough. Nobody cared as they concentrated on Billie's problem. "I want to spend more time with you kids," she said. "I want to get us going back to church on Sunday. I want to go to school at night, so I can get ahead."

"What about the money you're going to get for being a foster mother?" Jim asked. "Couldn't you use that?"

"That's to take care of you, and it's only temporary. I want to adopt you as soon as I can, make sure you stay here." She drew a deep breath. "There's one thing I could do. I could sell the house."

The shock of it silenced all of them for a moment. Then, "It's our home," Jennifer protested. "Lorraine was born here!"

"So I kill myself holding on to it and something happens that I can't keep up the payments, and I lose it anyway," Billie said. "Or I get my money out of it now, pay my bills, go to school, and we live in an apartment for a few years."

"Apartment living is the pits," Jennifer declared.

At the same time Lorraine asked, "Will it have a pool?"

"I'd try to stay in the same school district," Billie promised. "You'd still see your friends. The rent would be a lot less than my house payment. I could use that money to work less and go to school a couple nights a week. Nancy thinks if I go on to UCF and get my degree, I could even go to law school." The University of Central Florida was the local state university. "That's a long way down the road, after I get you kids through college, but I sure would like it."

128

"Couldn't we—?" Jennifer began, and changed her sentence. "If I give you all my baby-sitting money, and Jim gives you his lawn-mowing money, and Lorraine could baby-sit too if she'd just grow up, wouldn't that be enough?"

"You help out already by buying your own clothes," Billie said. "I need to get out from under this house." She looked at Jim. "How about you, Jim? What do you think?"

"I like it here."

"We all like it here," Billie said. "But I have to have more money, and it don't grow on trees." She flushed. "Okay, it *doesn't* grow on trees, so I made a mistake," she cried. "I guess I make a lot of them." None of them said anything. Billie's voice was strained when she spoke again. "Look," she said, "I'm not going to do anything in a hurry, but I can't keep on killing myself. Let's all think about it for a while."

Her mood infected all of them. For the rest of the evening they watched television and didn't talk. Jim hadn't felt so unhappy since the day his alligator killed Trudie.

# CHAPTER 19

I'm going to miss you, boy," Ben said when Jim
explained the situation the next afternoon.
"Patches'll miss you too." She ran in circles and tangled her leash around his legs. He laughed as he
untangled it. "One of these days she's going to
knock me down," he confided, "and then she'll be in
trouble."

His voice was full of affection for the little dog.
His life and his attention centered now on Patches;
he was pleased, rather than irritated, that she needed more from him than Trudie had. It was a fleeting
thought; at that moment Jim cared more about his
own needs than about Patches.

"I wouldn't be able to help you read your mail," he
complained.

"My daughter's coming next week," Ben replied.
"I'm getting my operation. But I'll sure miss you if
you stop coming around."

There was no comfort in the thought of being
missed. He didn't want to be missed, because he

didn't want to move. The injustice of it upset his balance as he rode his bike to Buddy's house.

"There wouldn't be anybody decent left on the street if you moved out," Buddy grumbled.

"What about me?" Jim cried. "I just got used to this place, now I have to start all over!"

"Maybe she won't be able to sell it," Buddy said hopefully. "My dad said houses aren't moving."

"You don't know my aunt," Jim retorted. "If she wants to do something, she does it."

It had always made him feel safe, Billie's determination to do what she thought was right. Now it threatened him. It wasn't fair, he thought as he rode home. He'd just settled in here, he shouldn't have to move again.

The next evening Troy drove Billie's car home.

"All I did was get it moving," he warned. "I worked on it on my own time, and Mr. Edelbert let me have the parts at cost. You don't have to pay me right away."

"I'll pay you while I have it," Billie said, and wrote him a check. "I really appreciate you helping me out."

"That car's not worth it," Troy said. "You find yourself a nice little car a couple years old, I'll check it out before you buy it."

"I'm thinking of selling my house," Billie said.

"Now you're talking. Get an apartment close to your work, take the bus, save the wear and tear on your car."

"This is our home," Jennifer cried, "and it's none of your business!"

"I guess not," Troy agreed, "but a home is the people in it, not a pile of cement blocks."

"He's right," Billie said later that evening, after she drove Troy back to the garage to pick up his truck. "It don't—doesn't—matter if we live in a house or an apartment as long as we're together. That's what's important."

"What about my lawns?" Jim asked.

"Maybe you'd find something else. Anyway I don't want you working except on weekends when school starts."

He was going to lose his lawn-mowing money during the winter even if they stayed there; Buddy had told him that the grass grew more slowly then, and most people cut their own.

"What about Ben?" he asked. "I'd never get to see him anymore."

"I'd see you didn't lose touch," Billie promised. "I'd try to live close enough so you could come over on your bike. And in a couple years you'll be driving."

Closer to three years, which was, in his mind, forever. The atmosphere in the house was gloomy. He and Jennifer were solidly against the move. Lorraine dismissed it from her mind except when they brought it up to her.

"Anything beyond the next five minutes is too

much for her to comprehend," Jennifer said sarcastically.

"Not," Lorraine contradicted. "Mom said she didn't make her mind up yet."

"She made up her mind the minute her car broke down on I-4," Jennifer said. "She's just trying to get us on her side."

Until then Jim had held out hope that they could change Billie's mind. Now he knew that Jennifer was right. They were going to move. Not right away; Billie had said that it would be hard to sell a house with two mortgages. But Nancy, her boss, was going to help her.

"I think it's her boss putting all these ideas in her head," he said.

"It's the only way she can get ahead," Jennifer replied. "I guess we have to go along with it."

He didn't want to go along with it. "Why doesn't she think about us?" he cried.

Even as he said it, before Jennifer replied, "She does. We have to think about her," he knew that he was being unfair. Billie always put the family first. Jim thought that he did too. Up to now it had been easy. What he'd wanted to do and what was good for the family were the same thing. Now there was a conflict.

"I want you to get ahead," he said to Billie when they were all around the table that weekend. "I just don't want to move."

"Isn't there some way we could keep the house and you could still go to school?" Jennifer begged.

"I don't think so, honey. I really messed up when I took out that second mortgage."

"You thought you were doing the right thing."

"I'm just sorry you kids have to suffer for it."

"I wouldn't say we're suffering," Jennifer countered. "We're upset, and we don't want to move, but I guess we know we have to do it."

"Jim?"

"I guess so."

So it was settled. They were sad, and short-tempered with one another. People were supposed to feel glad when they made a decision, even if they didn't like it, but Jim didn't feel glad. He thought of himself as being dragged out of this neighborhood and dumped down in a strange place. That's what happened to his gator. It must have felt terrified when it was hauled out of the water, thrown in a truck, and shooed into a lake out in the wilds of Florida.

At least he knew what was going to happen and why. The poor gator had only its instincts to guide it. But it survived. Deep inside him, he knew that he would too, even though he was still reluctant to admit it.

On Monday there was a letter in Billie's mail from Aunt Bessie. Jim recognized the large round handwriting even before he looked at the return address.

It must be his birth certificate. His spirits bumped up; at least one thing was going right.

As soon as she got home Billie opened the envelope and waved his birth certificate in the air. There was a letter accompanying it. "Aunt Bessie sold her house," she said after she read it. "She's going to a retirement home next week."

Somebody else moving, changing her life.

Billie felt inside the envelope again and took out a snapshot. "She heard from your daddy's folks in Georgia. They sent her a picture of your mother and daddy's wedding."

She handed him the photo. It was in color, of a woman in a white bridal gown and veil, and a man beside her in a dark suit. The woman was slight and fair and pretty, the man taller than his bride, and serious-looking. His hair was a carroty red and his ears stuck out. He wore heavy-rimmed glasses.

Jim stared at the picture. All sorts of emotions rose inside him; the sadness he felt when Grandma died, the apprehensions he had about moving from this house, the hope of his new life. He cleared his throat.

"My daddy looks just like me," he said.

The next day he showed the picture to Ben and Buddy, then bought a frame and put it in his room. Sleeping there night after night, he thought a lot about his parents, what kind of people they'd been, how they felt about things. His dad must have had trouble with the kids at school too, and probably wished, like Jim, that he was good-looking. But he lived through it. He married Jim's mother and they had a child and got on with their lives.

It was time to get on with his own. He lay in bed the night before school began and thought of all the things that happened to him that summer, and all the people who became part of his life. Billie and Jennifer and Lorraine, his new family. Ben, like a grandfather, and Trudie and Patches. Troy, sort of a big brother. His alligator, out in its lake, settled in by now.

He still wished that he hadn't fed it, and would always regret that Trudie died the way she did. But whenever there was a crisis in his life, his memories of that awful time helped him get through it. The day that it happened, he'd thought that he'd never be happy again. Knowing that his gator wasn't killed helped to ease the pain. Getting Patches for Ben, and finding out that the people he loved were willing to forgive him, did the rest. Sometimes you were lucky, and things turned out right.

He'd never forget his gator. Even when he was an old man he'd think of it, and tell his kids the story. But he knew now that he'd never drive out to Lake Nellie to look for it. Jennifer was right; he fed it to make himself feel better, with no thought for how his actions might affect the gator. He didn't need to go to Lake Nellie in order to make peace with himself, and the gators out there certainly didn't need a human being intruding on their peace and quiet.

It was the first night in weeks that he fell asleep without trying to decide what he'd answer when the kids at school called him ugly. When the time came, he'd think of something.